Maigret and the
Man On the Bench

Georges Simenon

Maigret and the
Man On the Bench

Translated from the French by Eileen Ellenbogen

A Harvest Book • Harcourt, Inc.

A Helen and Kurt Wolff Book

Orlando   Austin   New York   San Diego   Toronto   London

Library of Congress Cataloguing-in-Publication Data
Simenon, Georges, 1903–1989.
Maigret and the man on the bench.
(A Harvest book)
Translation of Maigret et l'homme du banc.
"A Helen and Kurt Wolff book."
I. Title.
PZ3.S5892Maegr 1979 [PQ2637.I53]
843'.9'12 78-13304
ISBN 0-15-602837-9

Printed in the United States of America
First Harvest edition 1979

A C E G I J H F D B

Maigret and the
Man On the Bench

CHAPTER ONE

THE
BROWN
SHOES

☐ Afterward, Maigret had no difficulty in recalling the date, October 29, because it happened also to be his sister-in-law's birthday. He even remembered the day, a Monday, since, as everyone at Quai des Orfèvres knows, murder is rarely committed on a Monday. And furthermore, as it happened, this case, unlike any other that year, had a flavor of winter about it.

A thin, cold drizzle had fallen all that Sunday, and the roads and pavements were black and glistening. A kind of yellowish fog seeped in through the chinks in the windows, so much so that Madame Maigret had said:

"Maybe I ought to get them fitted with draft stoppers."

For the past five years at least, as autumn approached, Maigret had been promising to fit them himself the following Sunday.

"You'd better wear your winter coat."

"Where is it?"

"I'll get it."

It was half past eight, still so dark that lights were on in all the houses, and Maigret's coat smelled of moth balls.

It did not rain that day, at least not noticeably, although

the pavements were still wet, and as the day wore on, and more and more people trampled them, they grew very slippery. Then, around four in the afternoon, the yellowish fog, which had cleared since morning, returned, blurring the light from the street lamps and windows.

When the telephone rang, neither Lucas nor Janvier nor even young Lapointe was in the inspector's office. It was answered by Santoni, a Corsican, who was new to the crime squad, having spent ten years first in the gaming squad and then in the vice squad.

"It's Inspector Neveu of the Third Arrondissement, Chief. He's asking to speak to you personally. He says it's urgent."

Maigret lifted the receiver.

"What is it, my boy?"

"I'm speaking from a bistro on Boulevard Saint-Martin. A man has just been found. He's been stabbed with a knife."

"Right there on the boulevard?"

"No, not quite. In a sort of blind alley."

Neveu, who was an old hand at this game, knew very well what Maigret must be thinking. There is seldom much of interest to the investigator in a stabbing. Usually, especially in overcrowded areas, it is the result of some drunken brawl or a quarrel between rival gangs of Spaniards or North Africans.

Neveu hastened to add:

"There are one or two odd features about this case. I think you ought to come and see for yourself. The alley runs between the big jeweler's and the artificial-flower shop."

"I'll come right away."

Maigret had never before worked on a case with Santoni. In the confined space of the little black police car, he was uncomfortably conscious of the powerful smell emanating from the Inspector, a little man, who wore high-heeled shoes. He used hair oil, and on his fourth finger wore a big yellow diamond, probably paste.

People flitted by like black shadows in the dark streets, and their shoes went flip-flap on the greasy pavements. On Boulevard Saint-Martin, two policemen wearing capes were holding back a crowd of some thirty people. Neveu, who was watching for Maigret, opened the door of the car.

"I persuaded the doctor to stay until you got here."

The Grands Boulevards are always jammed with people, but at this time of day the crowds were at their thickest. Above the jeweler's shop was a big clock. The hands on the illuminated dial stood at half past five. As for the artificial-flower shop, which had only one window, grimy and thick with dust, it was so dimly lighted and looked so neglected that one wondered if anyone ever went into it.

Between the two shops ran a little alley, so narrow as to be easily missed. It was no more than a gap between two walls, unlighted and apparently leading to the sort of paved courtyard to be found all over this district.

Neveu, followed by Maigret, elbowed his way through the crowd. A few yards inside the dark alley, several men were standing about. Two of them had flashlights. Their faces were a blur.

It was colder and damper here than on the boulevard. There was an unremitting draft. A dog, though roughly shoved aside by all and sundry, kept slinking back and getting under everyone's feet.

On the ground, against the dripping wall, lay a man, one arm bent under him, the other stretched out so that the ghostly hand almost touched the opposite wall, barring the way.

"Is he dead?"

The doctor, a local man, nodded.

"Death must have been instantaneous."

As if to underline these words, one of the flashlights played its circular beam back and forth over the corpse, throwing the projecting handle of the knife into eerie relief. The other one illuminated the man's profile, a staring eye, and a cheek grazed where he had scraped it against the wall as he fell.

"Who found the body?"

One of the uniformed men, who had been waiting for this opportunity, came forward. His features were barely visible. All one could tell was that he was young and distressed.

"I was on my rounds. I always take a quick look into all the little passages, because people get up to all sorts of beastliness in the dark in this kind of place. I saw someone lying on the ground. At first I thought it was a drunk."

"Already dead, was he?"

"Yes, I think so. But the body was still warm."

"What time was this?"

"A quarter to five. I blew my whistle, and as soon as reinforcements arrived I went off to telephone the station."

Neveu interposed:

"I took the call myself and came right over."

The local police station was only a few yards away, in Rue Notre-Dame-de-Nazareth.

Neveu went on:

"I left it to a colleague to call the doctor."

"Did no one hear anything?"

"Not as far as I know."

Maigret noticed a little farther on a door with a dimly lighted fanlight.

"Where does that lead?"

"Into the offices at the back of the jeweler's shop. It's hardly ever used."

Before leaving Quai des Orfèvres, Maigret had been in

touch with the Forensic Laboratory. The technicians had just arrived with their cameras and other equipment. Like all specialists, they concentrated solely on their job, asking no questions, worrying about nothing except how they were going to be able to manage in such a restricted space.

"Where does the courtyard lead to?" Maigret asked.

"Nowhere, just blank walls. There's only one door, which was condemned years ago, leading to a building on Rue Meslay."

The man, it was plain to see, had been stabbed in the back when he was ten paces or so inside the alley. Someone had silently crept in after him, and the crowds on the boulevard had streamed past unaware.

"I slipped my hand into his pocket and found this."

Neveu held out a wallet to Maigret. Without having to be asked, one of the men from Criminal Records shone a flashlight on it much more powerful than the Inspector's.

It was just an ordinary wallet, not new, but not particularly worn either. The best one could say of it was that it was of quite good quality. It contained three thousand-franc notes, a few of one hundred francs, and an identity card in the name of Louis Thouret, warehouse foreman, of 37 Rue des Peupliers, Juvisy. There were also a voter's registration card in the same name, a sheet of paper on which were scribbled five or six words in pencil, and a very old photograph of a little girl.

"Can we get started?"

Maigret nodded. Cameras clicked and bulbs flashed. The crowd at the entrance to the little passage was growing, and the police were having difficulty in holding them back.

Next, the technicians carefully withdrew the knife and put it in a special box. Only then did they turn the body over, to reveal the face of a man between forty and fifty, with a fixed expression of utter bewilderment.

He had been unable to understand what was happening

to him. He had died without understanding. There was something so childlike about his bewilderment, so incongruous in the tragic circumstances, that someone tittered nervously in the darkness.

His clothes were respectable and clean. He was wearing a dark three-piece suit and a beige spring coat, and his feet, oddly twisted, were encased in light-brown shoes, which seemed out of place on a day as somber as this.

Apart from his shoes, he was so ordinary looking that no one passing by in the street or sitting on one of the many café terraces on the boulevard would have spared him a second glance.

All the same, the policeman who had discovered the body remarked:

"I have a feeling I've seen him before."

"Where?"

"I can't remember, but the face seems familiar. I imagine he's one of those people you see around every day without really noticing them."

Neveu confirmed this.

"He looks vaguely familiar to me, too. Very likely he worked somewhere around here."

But that did not go anywhere toward explaining what Louis Thouret was doing in an alley leading nowhere. Maigret turned to Santoni, who had served for several years in the vice squad. For there are always a certain number of eccentrics with the best of reasons for lurking in lonely places, especially in this district. Nearly all are known to the police. Occasionally one of them proves to be a person of some prominence. From time to time they are arrested. As soon as they are released, they return to their old habits.

But Santoni shook his head.

"I've never seen him before."

Maigret's mind was made up.

"Carry on, men. When you've finished with him, have him sent to the Forensic Laboratory."

And to Santoni he said:

"We're going to see his family, if he has one."

If it had been an hour later, he would probably not have gone to Juvisy himself. But he had the car, and he was more than a little intrigued. The man was so utterly commonplace, a very ordinary man doing a very ordinary job.

"Let's be going, then, to Juvisy."

They stopped for a minute or two at the Porte d'Italie, to have a glass of beer standing at the bar. Then they sped along the expressway, dazzled by headlights, overtaking heavy trucks strung out nose to tail. When they reached the railway station at Juvisy, they had to ask five people before they found one able to direct them to Rue des Peupliers.

"It's part of the new housing development, right at the far end of town. When you get there, you'll just have to look at the street names. They're all called after trees, and they all look exactly alike."

They drove alongside the vast marshaling yard, where an endless stream of freight cars was being shunted into one siding or another. There were twenty engines, belching smoke, whistling and panting. Cars clashed together, shuddering on impact. On their right lay the new housing development, where building was still going on. The network of narrow streets was picked out in electric lights. There were hundreds, maybe thousands, of detached houses all exactly alike in size and shape. The noble trees after which the streets were named had not yet had time to grow. In some places the paving had not been completed, and the rough curbs were interspersed with black ditches. Elsewhere, on the other hand, there were neat little gardens in which the flowers of late autumn were begin-

ning to fade. Rue des Chênes ... Rue des Lilas ... Rue des
Hêtres. ... One day, maybe, it would look like one great park,
always provided the jerry-built houses, which were like units in
a toy construction set, didn't disintegrate before the trees
attained their full height.

Behind the kitchen windows, women were preparing
dinner. The streets were deserted, their uniformity broken here
and there by a little shop, brand-new, like everything else here,
and seemingly run by amateurs.

"Try the next turn on the left."

They went around in circles for ten minutes before finding
the street name they were looking for inscribed on a blue
plaque. They overshot the house, because number thirty-seven
came immediately after number twenty-one. There was only
one light showing, on the ground floor, in the kitchen. Through
the net curtains they could see the somewhat bulky figure of a
woman moving around.

"Let's go in," sighed Maigret, extricating himself with
some difficulty from the little car.

He emptied his pipe by tapping it on the heel of his shoe.
As they went toward the house, the curtain twitched, and they
caught a glimpse of a woman's face pressed against the window. Presumably a car parked at her door was an unusual sight
for her. Maigret went up the three front steps. The door was
of varnished pine, with wrought-iron trimmings and two small
panes of dark-blue glass. He looked for the bell, but before he
could find it a voice called out from the inside:

"What do you want?"

"Madame Thouret?"

"Yes?"

"I'd like a word with you."

She was still none too eager to open the door.

"It's police business," added Maigret, keeping his voice down.

At this, she slid back the chain and unbolted the door. Then, opening it a crack, through which only a narrow segment of her face could be seen, she looked searchingly at the two men waiting on the threshold.

"What is it you want?"

"I have something to tell you."

"How do I know you're really from the police?"

By the merest chance, Maigret happened to have his badge in his pocket. As a rule, he left it at home. He held it out to her so that it was illuminated by the beam of light from inside the house.

"Very well! It *is* genuine, I suppose?"

She let them in. The foyer was cramped, the walls were white, and the doors and doorframes were of varnished wood. The kitchen door had been left open, but she led them past it into the adjoining room. Having switched on the light, she ushered them in.

She was about the same age as her husband, but a good deal more heavily built, although she couldn't be called fat. It was her frame that was large, and covered in firm flesh. The gray dress she was wearing, protected by an apron, which she now mechanically took off, did nothing to soften her appearance.

The room to which she had taken them was a dining room furnished in rustic style. Presumably it was also used as a sitting room. There was a soulless tidiness about everything that was reminiscent of a window display or the interior of a furniture shop. Nothing had been left lying around, not even a pipe or a pack of cigarettes. There was not so much as a newspaper or a piece of needlework to be seen, nothing to suggest that people actually lived here. She did not ask them to sit down, but kept a wary eye on their feet, fearful lest they might dirty the linoleum.

"I'm listening."

"Your husband's name is Louis Thouret, is it not?"

She nodded, frowning as she tried to guess the purpose of their visit.

"Is his place of work in Paris?"

"He's assistant manager with the firm of Kaplan et Zanin, on Rue de Bondy."

"Has he ever worked as a warehouse foreman?"

"That used to be his job."

"How long ago?"

"Some years. Even then, he was the one who really kept the business going."

"Have you, by any chance, a photograph of him?"

"What do you want it for?"

"I want to be sure . . ."

"Sure of what?"

She was becoming more and more suspicious.

"Has Louis had an accident?"

Mechanically she glanced at the clock, and then frowned, as if trying to recall where her husband would be at this time of day.

"I'd like to satisfy myself that he is the man in question."

"On the sideboard," she said.

There were five or six photographs in metal frames on the sideboard, one of a young girl standing beside the man who had been found stabbed in the alley. He looked a good deal younger, and was dressed in black.

"Do you know if your husband had any enemies?"

"Why on earth should he have enemies?"

She went out for a moment, to turn down the gas under a saucepan that was bubbling on the stove.

"What time does he usually get back from work?"

"He always catches the same train, the 6:22 from the Gare de Lyon. Our daughter comes on the train after that, because she finishes work a little later than he does. She has a very responsible job . . ."

"I'm afraid I'll have to ask you to return with me to Paris."

"Is Louis dead?"

She looked him up and down, defying him to lie to her.

"I want the truth."

"He was murdered this afternoon."

"Where did it happen?"

"In a little passage off Boulevard Saint-Martin."

"What was he doing there?"

"I've no idea."

"What time was it?"

"As far as we can tell, around half past four."

"At half past four he's still at work. Have you inquired at Kaplan's?"

"There hasn't been time. And, besides, we didn't know where he worked."

"Who killed him?"

"That's what we are trying to find out."

"Was he alone?"

Maigret was beginning to lose patience.

"Don't you think you'd better get ready? The sooner we leave, the better."

"What have you done with him?"

"By this time, he will have been taken to the Forensic Laboratory."

"The morgue, you mean."

What could he say to that?

"My daughter will have to be told."

"You could leave her a note."

She considered this.

"No. We'd better stop by my sister's. I'll leave the key with her. She can come over and wait for Monique here. Will you be wanting to talk to her, as well?"

"I would like to, yes."

"Where should she meet us?"

"In my office at Quai des Orfèvres. It would save a lot of time. How old is she?"

"Twenty-two."

"Couldn't you give her a ring and break the news to her yourself?"

"Well, for one thing, I don't have a telephone, and, for another, she'll have left her office and will be on her way to the station by now. I won't keep you long."

She went up the stairs, which creaked at every step, not because they were old, but because they were constructed of flimsy planks of wood. It was obvious that the house and everything in it had been cheaply built. Doubtless it would not survive to be old.

The two men exchanged glances as they listened to the comings and goings overhead. She was changing into a black dress, they were sure, and probably brushing her hair. When she came downstairs, they once more exchanged glances. They had been right. She was already wearing mourning, and smelled of eau de cologne.

"Would you wait for me outside while I switch off the lights and the gas?"

She looked doubtfully at the little car, as if afraid that there wouldn't be room for her. Someone was watching them from the house next door.

"My sister lives just two streets away. Go right at the next turn, driver, and then it's the second on the left."

The two little houses were identical, except that the panels of glass in the door were a different color here, apricot instead of blue.

"I won't be a moment."

But she was gone about a quarter of an hour. When she returned to the car, she had another woman with her, who was also dressed in black, and who was so like her in every way that they might have been twins.

"My sister is coming with us. I daresay we'll manage to squeeze in somehow. My brother-in-law will go to my house and wait for my daughter. It's his day off. He's an inspector on the railroad."

Maigret sat next to the driver. Santoni and the two women squeezed uncomfortably into the back. The sisters could be heard whispering to each other from time to time, as if in the confessional.

When they got to the Forensic Laboratory, near the Pont d'Austerlitz, they found the body of Louis Thouret still fully clothed, in accordance with Maigret's instructions. He was laid out temporarily on a marble slab. It was Maigret, his eyes on the two women, who uncovered the face. It was the first time he had seen them together in a good light. At first, in the darkened street, he had mistaken them for twins. Now he could see that the sister was three or four years younger, her figure having retained a measure of suppleness, though probably not for long.

"Do you recognize him?"

Madame Thouret, with a handkerchief crumpled in her hand, did not weep. Her sister took her by the arm, desirous of offering comfort and support.

"Yes, that's Louis. That's my poor Louis. I'm sure he

never dreamed, when he left the house this morning . . ."

She broke off abruptly to say:

"Why are his eyes still open?"

"You may close them now, if you wish."

She and her sister exchanged glances, as though uncertain which of them should undertake the task. In the end, it was the widow who did it, with ritual solemnity, murmuring:

"Poor Louis."

Then, all of a sudden, she caught sight of the shoes projecting beyond the sheet covering the body. She frowned.

"What's this?"

Maigret couldn't imagine what she was talking about.

"Who put those shoes on him?"

"He was wearing them when we found him."

"It's not possible. Louis never wore brown shoes. At any rate, never during the twenty-six years that we were married. As he very well knew, I wouldn't have permitted it. Do you see, Jeanne?"

Jeanne nodded.

"I think perhaps you'd better make sure the clothes he is wearing are his own. I take it you are in no doubt as to his identity?"

"None whatever. But those are not his shoes. I should know. I polish them every day. When he left this morning, he was wearing black shoes, the pair with the reinforced soles that he always wore to work."

Maigret removed the sheet.

"Is this his overcoat?"

"Yes."

"And his suit?"

"Yes, that's his. But that isn't his tie. He would never have worn anything so garish. Why, you could almost call it red!"

"Was your husband a man of regular habits?"

"He certainly was. Ask my sister. Every morning he caught the bus at the corner, which got him to Juvisy station in time to catch the 8:17 train. He always traveled with our neighbor Monsieur Beaudoin, who works in Inland Revenue. From the Gare de Lyon, they went on to Saint-Martin by Métro."

The employee of the Forensic Laboratory made a sign to Maigret. Realizing what was required of him, he led the two women toward a table on which the contents of the dead man's pockets had been laid out.

"I take it you recognize these things?"

There were a silver watch and chain, a plain handkerchief without initials, an open pack of Gauloise cigarettes, a lighter, a key, and, lying beside the man's wallet, a couple of bluish ticket stubs.

The first things that caught the widow's eye were the ticket stubs.

"Those are movie tickets," she said.

Maigret examined them and said:

"A newsreel movie on Boulevard Bonne-Nouvelle. The figures are a bit rubbed, but, as far as I can see, they were issued today."

"That's not possible. Did you hear that, Jeanne?"

"It does seem odd," said her sister, without emotion.

"Would you please take a look at the contents of the wallet."

She did so, and frowned.

"Louis didn't have as much money as this on him when he left this morning."

"Are you sure?"

"I always see to it myself that he has money in his wallet. At most, he had a thousand-franc note and two or three hundred-franc notes."

"Couldn't he perhaps have collected his pay?"

"He didn't get paid till the end of the month."

"How much did he usually have left at the end of the day?"

"All of it, less the price of his Métro ticket and his cigarettes. He had a season ticket for the train."

She seemed about to put the wallet in her bag, but thought better of it.

"I daresay you'll want to keep this for a while?"

"For the time being, yes."

"What puzzles me is why they should have changed his shoes and tie. And what he was doing away from the shop at the time it happened."

Maigret, not wishing to harass her, asked no further questions, but merely handed her the necessary forms to sign.

"Are you going straight home?"

"When can we have the body?"

"In a day or two, I should think."

"Will there have to be a post-mortem?"

"That's up to the examining magistrate. He may not think it necessary."

She glanced at her watch.

"There's a train in twenty minutes," she said to her sister. And to Maigret:

"Would you mind taking us to the station?"

"Don't you want to wait for Monique?"

"She can make her own way."

The Gare de Lyon was a good deal out of their way. They watched the two almost identical figures going up the stone steps.

Gruffly, Santoni said: "She's as hard as nails! The poor fellow can't have had much of a life."

"Not with her, at any rate."

"What do you make of that business of the shoes? The

obvious answer would be that he bought them today, except that they aren't new."

"He wouldn't have dared. You heard what she said."

"He wouldn't have dared to buy a loud tie either."

"It will be interesting to see whether the daughter is like her mother."

Before returning to Quai des Orfèvres, they stopped to eat at a brasserie. Maigret telephoned his wife, to tell her to expect him when she saw him.

The brasserie, too, smelled of winter, with damp coats and hats hanging from all the hooks and dense clouds of steam rising from the dark windows.

At the gatehouse to Police Headquarters Maigret was met by the man on duty, who announced:

"There's a young woman waiting to see you. She says she has an appointment. I sent her straight up."

"Has she been here long?"

"Twenty minutes or so."

The fog had turned to a thin drizzle, and the dusty treads of the main staircase were intricately patterned with damp footprints. Although most of the offices were empty, here and there a crack of light showed under a door.

"Do you want me to stay?"

Maigret nodded. Santoni had been with him on the case from the start. He might as well see it through to the end.

There was a young woman sitting in an armchair in the waiting room, though all that could be seen of her was a pale-blue hat. There was only one dim light on in the room. The desk clerk was reading an evening paper.

"She's waiting to see you, Chief."

"I know."

And to the young woman:

"Mademoiselle Thouret? Will you come with me, please?"

He switched on the green-shaded light that hung above the chair across the desk from his own and invited her to take a seat. She did so, and he could see that she had been crying.

"My uncle has told me of my father's death."

He did not say anything at first. Like her mother, she had a handkerchief in her hand, but hers was rolled into a ball and she was kneading it, as Maigret used to knead clay when he was a child.

"I thought my mother would be with you."

"She's gone back to Juvisy."

"How is she?"

What could he say?

"Your mother was very brave."

Monique was not unattractive. She did not look much like her mother, although she was of the same heavy build. This was less marked in her case because her young skin was softer and her body more supple. She was wearing a well-cut suit. The Chief Superintendent found this a little surprising. She had certainly not made it herself, nor had it been bought in a cheap shop.

A few drops of moisture gathered on her eyelashes as she asked:

"What happened exactly?"

"Your father was stabbed with a knife."

"When?"

"This afternoon, between half past four and a quarter to five."

"I simply can't understand it."

Why was it that he had a feeling she was not being altogether sincere? Her mother, too, had expressed incredulity, but, being the sort of woman she was, that was only to be expected. Basically, as far as Madame Thouret was concerned, it was a disgraceful thing to get oneself murdered in an alleyway off

Boulevard Saint-Martin. She had planned her life in every detail, not only her life, but also that of her family, and murder had no place in her scheme of things—especially this murder, with the corpse wearing brown shoes and a tie that might almost be described as red!

As for Monique, though she seemed on the whole a sensible girl, she was obviously apprehensive. There would be questions that she would prefer not to answer and revelations that she would prefer not to hear.

"Did you know your father well?"

"But . . . of course."

"Of course you knew him in the way that most children know their parents. What I mean is, were you and he in each other's confidence? Did he ever talk to you about his private life and private thoughts?"

"He was a good father."

"Was he a happy man?"

"I suppose so."

"Did you and he ever meet in town?"

"I don't understand. Do you mean did we ever run into each other in the street?"

"You both worked in Paris. I know you didn't go to work or return home on the same train."

"We kept different office hours."

"You might have met for lunch occasionally."

"We did, sometimes."

"Often?"

"No, not very often."

"Did you go and pick him up at the shop?"

She hesitated.

"No. We would meet in some restaurant or other."

"Did you ever telephone him at work?"

"Not as far as I can remember."

"When did you last meet for lunch?"

"Several months ago. Before the summer holidays."

"Whereabouts?"

"At La Chope Alsacienne, on Boulevard Sébastopol."

"Did you mother know?"

"I daresay I mentioned it to her. I don't remember."

"Was your father of a cheerful disposition?"

"Fairly cheerful, I think."

"How was his health?"

"I've never known him to be ill."

"Had he many friends?"

"We saw hardly anyone, apart from my aunts and uncles."

"Have you many?"

"Two aunts and two uncles."

"Do they all live in Juvisy?"

"Yes. Not very far from us. It was my uncle Albert, my aunt Jeanne's husband, who told me of my father's death. My aunt Céline's house is a little farther away."

"Are they both sisters of your mother?"

"Yes. And Aunt Céline's husband, my uncle Julien, also works for the railroad."

"Is there a man in your life, Mademoiselle Monique?"

She looked a little flustered.

"Surely this is no time to go into that. Don't you want me to see my father?"

"What do you mean?"

"I understood from my uncle that I would be required to identify his body."

"Your mother and your aunt have already done that. However, if you wish to . . ."

"No. I suppose I'll see him when he's brought home."

"Just one more thing, Mademoiselle Monique. When you

met your father in town for lunch, can you remember if you ever saw him wearing brown shoes?"

She didn't answer at once. To gain time, she repeated:

"Brown shoes?"

"Well, very light brown would perhaps be a better description. What in my day, if you'll pardon the expression, used to be called goose-dung shoes."

"I can't remember."

"Did you ever see him wearing a red tie?"

"No."

"When did you last go to the movies?"

"Yesterday afternoon."

"Here, in town?"

"In Juvisy."

"I won't keep you any longer. I hope you haven't missed the last train."

"It leaves in thirty-five minutes."

She glanced at her wrist watch and stood up. There was a pause.

"Good night," she said at last.

"Good night, mademoiselle, and thank you."

Maigret went to the door with her and closed it behind her.

CHAPTER TWO

THE
PUG-NOSED
VIRGIN

☐ Maigret, though he could not say why, had always had a special affection for the section of the Grands Boulevards that stretches from Place de la République to Rue Montmartre. To put it another way, he felt that he was on home ground. It was here, on Boulevard Bonne-Nouvelle, just a few hundred yards from the passageway in which Louis Thouret had been killed, that Maigret and his wife went to a movie almost every week. Arm in arm, they walked the short distance from their apartment to what they regarded as their local movie house. And opposite was the brasserie where he enjoyed going for a dish of *choucroute*.

Farther on, approaching the Opéra and the Madeleine, the boulevards were more spacious and elegant. In the area between Porte Saint-Martin and Place de la République the streets were narrower and darker, and so densely packed with people on the move as to make one feel dizzy.

He had left home at about half past eight and, walking at a leisurely pace in the gray morning light, had taken barely a quarter of an hour to reach the intersection of Rue de Bondy and the boulevard, which formed a little square dominated by the Théâtre de la Renaissance. The weather was less damp than on the previous day, but colder. Maigret was looking for the premises of the firm of Kaplan et Zanin, where, according to Louis Thouret's wife, he had spent the whole of his working life, including his last day on earth.

The number Maigret had been given was that of a very old building, visibly subsiding. On either side of the gateway, which was wide open, were a number of white enamel plaques with black lettering, indicating that among the tenants were a mattress maker, a secretarial college, a wholesaler in feathers (third floor on the left, Staircase A), an upholsterer, and a qualified masseuse. The concierge in the lodge, which faced the archway, was engaged in sorting the mail.

"Could you please direct me to Kaplan et Zanin?" he asked her.

"My dear sir, they closed down three years ago, three years next month."

"Were you here then?"

"I will have been here twenty-six years in December."

"Did you know Louis Thouret?"

"Know him? Why, of course I knew Monsieur Louis. By the way, what has become of him? It must be all of four or five months since he last stopped in to say hello to me."

"He's dead."

Abruptly, she pushed the letters aside.

"But he was such a healthy man! What did he die of? A heart attack, I'll be bound, the same as my husband."

"He was stabbed with a knife, not far from here, yesterday afternoon."

"I haven't seen the paper today."

Anyway, there was nothing much in the papers, just a few terse lines reporting the murder, as if it were an everyday occurrence.

"Whoever could have wanted to kill a fine man like him?"

She was a worthy soul herself, a little creature, but full of life.

"For more than twenty years, he went past this lodge four times a day, and never once did he fail to stop and say a pleasant word or two. When Monsieur Kaplan gave up the business, he was so shattered that . . ."

She had to stop to wipe her eyes and blow her nose.

"Is Monsieur Kaplan still alive?"

"I can give you his address if you like. He lives in Rue des Acacias, near Porte Maillot. He's a fine man, too, in his own way. I believe old Monsieur Kaplan is still alive."

"What did the firm deal in?"

"You mean you don't know?"

She seemed to think that the whole world ought to have heard of the firm of Kaplan et Zanin. Maigret explained:

"I'm from the police. I have to find out all I can about Monsieur Thouret and anything to do with him."

"We always called him Monsieur Louis. Everybody did. Most people didn't even know his surname. If you wouldn't mind waiting a moment . . ."

She returned to the mail, murmuring to herself, as she sorted the last few letters:

"Monsieur Louis murdered! I wouldn't have believed it possible. A man of such . . ."

Having slotted the letters into the various pigeonholes, she wrapped a woolen shawl around her shoulders and turned down the coal stove.

"Come and I'll show you."

When they were under the archway, she explained:

"This building was due to be torn down three years ago, to make way for a movie theater. At that time, the tenants were given notice, and I myself made arrangements to go and live with my daughter in the Nièvre region. That was the reason Monsieur Kaplan gave up the business. Though the fact that business was none too brisk may also have had something to do with it. Young Monsieur Kaplan, Monsieur Max, as we called him, didn't see eye to eye with his father. This way . . ."

Beyond the archway was a courtyard, at the end of which could be seen a large building with a glass roof that looked like the concourse of a railroad station. On the roughcast wall only a few letters of the name *Kaplan et Zanin* were still legible.

"There were no longer any Zanins in the firm when I came to this place twenty-six years ago. At that time, old Monsieur Kaplan was running the business singlehanded. Children would stop in the street and stare at him, because he had the look of an Old Testament patriarch."

The door was not shut. The lock had been wrenched out. Everything around them was now in decay, though a few years earlier it had been part of a living world, the world of Louis Thouret. What, precisely, the place had been used for, it was hard to tell. It was a huge room, rising to a very high glass roof, the panes of which were now either missing or opaque with grime. Two galleries, one above the other, such as are often to be seen in big stores, ran right around the room, and there were marks on the walls where there had once been rows of shelves.

"Whenever he came to see me . . ."

"Did he come often?"

"Every two or three months, I'd say, and he never came empty-handed. And each time, let me tell you, Monsieur Louis insisted on coming in here to take a look around, and you could tell that his heart was heavy. I've known there to be as many as twenty girl packers in here, even more toward the end, and especially at Christmas time, and quite often they worked late into the night. This wasn't a retail business. Monsieur Kaplan sold direct to the cheap variety stores up and down the country, and to market traders of all sorts. There was so much stuff in here that you could scarcely move. Monsieur Louis was the only one who knew where everything was. Heaven knows, there was variety enough, false beards, cardboard trumpets, Christmas tree decorations of every sort, paper streamers, carnival masks, and seaside resort souvenirs."

"Was Monsieur Louis in charge of the stock?"

"Yes. He always wore gray overalls. Over there in the right-hand corner—see?—Monsieur Kaplan sat in his glass-walled office. The young Monsieur Kaplan, I mean, after his father had his first heart attack and stopped coming in. He had a secretary, Mademoiselle Léone, and an elderly bookkeeper, who worked in a little cubbyhole upstairs. No one had the least inkling of what was in store for them. One day, without warning—I'm not sure exactly when, but it must have been in October or November, because there was a nip in the air already—Monsieur Max Kaplan called his staff together, and told them that the firm was to be closed down and that he had found a buyer for the stock.

"Everyone believed at the time that the building was to come down the following year, to make way for a movie house, as I told you."

Maigret listened patiently, looking about him and trying to picture the scene in all its former glory.

"The front part of the building is due for demolition, as well. All the tenants have been given notice. Some have already left. The others have hung on, and, as things have turned out, they made the right decision, seeing that they're still here. The only trouble is that since the building was sold the new owners have refused to maintain it. There are goodness knows how many lawsuits pending. The bailiff turns up once a month or so. I've packed up all my things twice already."

"Do you know Madame Thouret?"

"I've never set eyes on her. They lived in the suburbs, in Juvisy."

"She's still there."

"Have you met her? What's she like?"

Maigret's only reply was a grimace, leaving her in no doubt as to his feelings.

"I'm not surprised. I had a feeling that he wasn't particularly happy in his home life. His real life was here. I've always said that when the blow fell he was the hardest hit of all. Especially when you think that he was at the age when it's difficult to change the habits of a lifetime."

"How old was he?"

"Forty-five or forty-six, I'd say."

"Do you know what he did after he left here?"

"He never spoke about it. He must have been through some hard times. For a long time after he left, I didn't see him. Then one day I was out shopping, in a tearing hurry as usual, and I caught sight of him sitting on a bench. It was a shock. You just wouldn't expect to see a man like him idle in the middle of the day. I was on the point of going up to him when it struck me that it could only cause him embarrassment, so I turned off into a side street."

"How long was this after the business closed down?"

It was even colder here under the glass roof than in the courtyard.

"Would you like to come into the lodge and warm up?" she suggested. "It's hard to say how long after. It wasn't in the spring. There were no leaves on the trees. It was probably just about the end of winter."

"When was the next time you saw him?"

"Oh, long afterward, in midsummer. The thing that struck

me most was that he was wearing goose-dung shoes. Why are you looking at me like that?"

"No reason. Please go on."

"It was so out of character. He always wore black shoes when he worked here. He came into the lodge and put a small parcel down on the table. It was wrapped in white paper and tied with gold ribbon. It was a box of chocolates. He sat down in this chair here. I made him a cup of coffee and slipped out to get a half bottle of Calvados from the shop on the corner, leaving him to keep an eye on things in the lodge."

"What did he have to say for himself?"

"Nothing special. But you could see that it made him happy just to be breathing the air of this place again."

"Didn't he refer to the change in his life?"

"I asked him how things were going, and he said he had nothing to complain of. At any rate, he obviously wasn't working office hours, seeing that he was able to call on me between ten and eleven in the morning. Another time, he came in the afternoon, and he was wearing a light-colored tie. I teased him about it and remarked that it made him look years younger. He was never one to take offense. Then I asked about his daughter. I've never met her, but he always carried photographs of her, right from the time she was a few months old. He was a proud father, all right, and was always ready to show the photographs to anyone."

No recent photographs of Monique had been found on him, only the one taken when she was a baby.

"Is that all you can tell me?"

"How would I know anything more? I'm shut up in this place from morning to night. Since Kaplan's closed down and the hairdresser on the first floor left, things haven't been any too lively here."

"Did you and he talk about that?"

"Yes. We chatted about all sorts of things, such as the number of tenants who had moved out, one after another, the lawsuits, the architects who came in from time to time studying the plans for their wretched movie, while the walls slowly crumbled in ruins around us."

She did not sound bitter. All the same, he was sure that she would hang on long after everyone else had left.

"How did it happen?" she asked in her turn. "Did he suffer much?"

Neither Madame Thouret nor Monique had thought to put this question to him.

"The doctor says not. Apparently he died instantly."

"Where did it happen?"

"Not very far from here, in an alleyway off Boulevard Saint-Martin."

"Near the jeweler's, do you mean?"

"Yes. Someone must have been following him in the dusk. At any rate, he was found with a knife in his back."

Maigret had telephoned the Forensic Laboratory from his home the previous night and again this morning. The knife was a very ordinary mass-produced article, to be found on the shelves of almost any hardware shop. It was new, and there were no fingerprints on it.

"Poor Monsieur Louis! He did so enjoy life."

"You mean he was always cheerful?"

"It's hard to explain. He certainly wasn't an unhappy man. He always had a smile and a kind word for everyone. He was very considerate, and modest besides."

"Did he seem interested in women?"

"Never! And yet there were plenty of opportunities here. Apart from Monsieur Max and the old bookkeeper, he was the only man around, and women who take jobs as packers aren't exactly strait-laced, as a rule."

"Did he drink?"

"Just a glass of wine, like anyone else. Occasionally he would have a liqueur with his coffee."

"Where did he go for lunch?"

"He hardly ever went out. He nearly always brought sandwiches wrapped in waxed paper. I can see him now. He ate standing up, with his package of sandwiches open on the table. Afterward, he would go out into the courtyard and smoke his pipe before returning to the stockroom. Very occasionally he would go out, announcing to me that he was having lunch with his daughter. This was toward the end of his time here. His daughter was quite grown up by then and had an office job in Rue de Rivoli.

"'Why not bring her back here, Monsieur Louis? I would so love to meet her.'

"'I will one day . . .' he promised.

"But he never did. I've often wondered why."

"Have you lost touch with Mademoiselle Léone?"

"No, indeed. In fact, I have her address. She lives with her mother. She doesn't work in an office any more. She's opened a little shop in Rue de Clignancourt in Montmartre. She may be able to tell you more than I can. He used to go and see her, too. On one occasion, when we were talking about her, he told me that she was selling layettes and all sorts of other things for babies. It seems odd, somehow."

"What's odd about it?"

"That she, of all people, should be selling things for babies."

People were beginning to come into the lodge to collect their mail. They looked at Maigret uneasily, assuming, no doubt, that he, like others before him, had come to evict them.

"Thanks for your help. I'll be back before very long, I daresay."

"Have you any idea who might have done it?"

"None," he frankly admitted.

"Was his wallet stolen?"

"No, nor his watch."

"Well, then he must have been mistaken for someone else."

Rue de Clignancourt was in another part of the city. Maigret went into a little bar and made straight for the telephone booth.

"Who's speaking?"

"Janvier here, Chief."

"Any news?"

"In accordance with your instructions, the men are already out on the job."

These were the five inspectors, each assigned to a different district, who had been detailed to comb all the hardware shops in Paris. As for Santoni, Maigret had instructed him to find out everything he could about Monique Thouret. By now he must be in Rue de Rivoli sniffing around the offices of Geber et Bachelier, Solicitors.

If Madame Thouret had had a telephone, Maigret would have called her in Juvisy to ask whether, during the past three years, her husband had continued to leave home every morning with his lunch wrapped in a square of waxed paper.

"I'd be glad if you'd send a car for me."

"Where are you?"

"In Rue de Bondy. Tell the driver I'll be waiting across from the Théâtre de la Renaissance."

He was on the point of instructing Janvier, who for once was not snowed under with work, to assist with the inquiries among the shopkeepers on Boulevard Saint-Martin. Inspector

Neveu was already on the job, but with work of that sort extra help was always appreciated.

Then he thought better of it, mainly because he had an urge to return to the district himself.

"Any other instructions?"

"I want photographs sent to all the newspapers. They've played down the story so far, and I'd be grateful if they'd keep it that way."

"I get it. I'll send you a car right away."

Partly because the concierge happened to have mentioned Calvados, and partly because of the extreme cold, Maigret ordered a glass before he left the bar. Then, with his hands in his pockets, he crossed over to the boulevard to have another look at the alley where Monsieur Louis had been found stabbed.

So reticent had the newspapers been on the subject of the murder that not a single one of the passers-by stopped to peer at the paving stones in the hope of finding traces of blood.

He stood for quite a time gazing into one of the two display windows of the jeweler's shop. Inside, he could see five or six assistants of both sexes. The jewelry was, for the most part, second-rate stuff. Many of the pieces on view were described as "Bargain Offers." Both windows were crammed with goods: wedding rings, paste diamonds and possibly one or two genuine ones, alarm clocks, watches, and hideous mantel clocks.

A little old man, who had been watching Maigret for some time from inside the shop, must have decided that he was a potential customer, since he came to the door with a smile on his face, intending to invite him in. But the Chief Superintendent thought it was time he took himself off, and walked back toward the spot where the Headquarters car was waiting for him.

"Rue de Clignancourt," he said to the driver.

It was a good deal quieter than Boulevard Saint-Martin, but

this, too, was a district of small tradespeople, and Mademoiselle Léone's shop—from the sign above it, he gathered it was called Le Bébé Rose—was so completely eclipsed by a horsemeat butcher's on one side and a cabmen's eating place on the other that one would have to be an initiate to find it.

Going into the shop, he could see in the back room an old woman in an armchair, with a cat on her lap. Another, younger woman came forward to meet him. He looked at her with a silent sense of shock. She did not conform to his preconceived notion of what a secretary who had worked for the firm of Kaplan should look like. What was it about her? he wondered. He could not say. Presumably she was wearing felt slippers, since her footsteps made no sound. For this reason, she reminded him a little of a nun, and her deportment also was that of a nun, for she advanced seemingly without moving her body.

She wore a faint smile, which was not confined to her mouth but played about all her features. She had a very gentle expression and a self-effacing manner.

How strange that she should be called Léone, the more so as she had a broad pug nose such as one might see on an aged lion slumbering in a cage.

"What can I do for you, Monsieur?"

She was dressed in black. Her face and hands were colorless, ethereal. Comforting gusts of warmth blew into the shop from the big stove in the back room, and everywhere, on the shelves and on the counter, there were fragile knitted garments, bootees threaded with pink or blue ribbons, bonnets, christening robes.

"I am Chief Superintendent Maigret of the Police Judiciaire."

"Oh?"

"I have to inform you that Louis Thouret, a former colleague of yours, I believe, was murdered yesterday."

No one else had taken the news to heart as she did. And yet she didn't cry, or fumble for a handkerchief, or screw up her face. The shock of it froze her where she stood and for a moment, he could have sworn, arrested the beating of her heart. And he saw her lips, which were pale anyway, turn as white as the baby clothes all around her.

"Please forgive me. I ought not to have put it so bluntly."

She shook her head, wishing him to understand that she did not hold it against him. The old lady in the back room stirred.

"If I am to find his murderer, I need to learn everything there is to be known about him."

She nodded, but still did not speak.

"I believe you knew him well?"

For an instant her face lighted up.

"How did it happen?" she finally asked, with a lump in her throat.

She must have been ugly even as a little girl, and no doubt she had always been conscious of the fact. Glancing toward the other room, she murmured:

"I'm sure you'd be more comfortable sitting down."

"I don't think your mother . . ."

"We can talk freely in front of Mother. She's stone-deaf. But she does like company."

He could not possibly have admitted to her that he felt suffocated in this airless room where the two women spent the greater part of their cramped existence.

Léone was ageless. In all probability, she was over fifty, perhaps a lot older than that. Her mother looked all of eighty, as she darted a glance at the Chief Superintendent with her bright little birdlike eyes. It was not from her that Léone had inherited her broad pug nose, but from her father, if the enlarged photograph on the wall was anything to go by.

"I've just come from seeing the concierge in Rue de Bondy."

"It must have been a great shock to her."

"Yes. She was very fond of him."

"Everyone was."

She colored a little as she spoke.

"He was such a good man!" she hastened to add.

"You saw quite a lot of him, isn't that so?"

"He came to see me several times. You couldn't say I saw him often. He was a very busy man, and he lived a long way out of town."

"Do you happen to know how he had been spending his time recently?"

"I never asked him. He seemed to be doing well. I presumed he was self-employed, since he didn't have to keep office hours."

"Did he never talk to you about the people he met?"

"We mostly reminisced about Rue de Bondy, and Kaplan's and Monsieur Max, and taking inventory. What an upheaval that used to be every year, with more than a thousand different lines in stock."

She hesitated.

"I presume you've seen his wife?"

"Yesterday evening, yes."

"How did she take it?"

"She couldn't understand how her husband came to be wearing light-brown shoes when he was killed. She claims that the murderer must have put them on him."

Léone, like the concierge, had noticed the shoes.

"No. He often wore them."

"Even when he was working in Rue de Bondy?"

"No, only after he left. Some time after."

"How long after?"

"About a year."

"Did it surprise you that he should be wearing light-brown shoes?"

"Yes. It was different from his usual style of dress."

"What did you think about it?"

"That he had changed."

"Did you notice any actual change in him?"

"He wasn't quite the same man. His sense of fun had changed. Sometimes he laughed as if he would never stop."

"Didn't he ever laugh in the old days?"

"Not in that way. Something new had come into his life."

"A woman?"

It was cruel, but he had to ask.

"Perhaps."

"Did he never confide in you?"

"No."

"Did he ever make love to you?"

Vehemently, she protested:

"Never! I swear it! I'm sure no such thought ever entered his head."

The cat had abandoned the old lady, to jump up onto Maigret's lap.

"Let it stay," he said, as Léone seemed about to shoo it off.

He didn't have the courage to light his pipe.

"I daresay it was a bitter blow to you all when Monsieur Kaplan announced that he was about to close down the business?"

"We were all hard hit, yes."

"And especially Louis Thouret?"

"Monsieur Louis was particularly attached to the firm. It had become a habit with him. Just think of it, he'd been working there from the age of fourteen, when he started as a messenger boy."

"Where was he from?"

"From Belleville. From what he told me, his mother was a widow. She brought him in one day to see old Monsieur Kaplan. He was still in short pants. He had had practically no schooling."

"Is his mother dead?"

"She has been for many years."

Why was it that Maigret had the feeling she was hiding something? She had spoken freely and had looked him straight in the eye, and yet there was something evasive about her, as though she were gliding furtively away from him on silent, felt-shod feet.

"I believe he had some difficulty in finding another job?"

"Who told you that?"

"I gathered it from some of the things the concierge told me."

"It's never easy for someone over forty to find work, particularly if he has no special qualifications. I myself . . ."

"Did you look for a job?"

"Only for a few weeks."

"And Monsieur Louis?"

"He persisted longer."

"Is that just a supposition, or do you actually know he did?"

"I know he did."

"Did he ever come and see you during that period?"

"Yes."

"Did you help him financially?"

He was by now convinced that Léone was the sort of person to have saved every penny she could.

"Why do you want to know?"

"Because, until I have a clear picture of the kind of man

he was during the last few years of his life, I have no hope of laying my hand on his murderer."

"It's true," she admitted, after a pause for thought. "I'll tell you the whole story, but I'd be grateful if you would keep it to yourself. Above all, his wife mustn't find out. It would be a bitter blow to her pride."

"Do you know her, then?"

"No, he told me. His brothers-in-law both have responsible jobs, and both had built new homes."

"So did he."

"He had no choice; his wife had set her heart on it. She was the one who insisted on moving to Juvisy, like her two sisters."

Her voice had somehow changed, and one could sense the underlying rancor that must have been festering for a long time.

"Was he afraid of his wife?"

"He hated to hurt anyone. When we all got the sack, a few weeks before the Christmas holidays, he was determined to see that it didn't spoil the family festivities."

"You mean he didn't say anything to them, but just let them go on believing that he was still working in Rue de Bondy?"

"He thought at first it would only be a matter of days before he got another job. Later, he thought it might take weeks. The only thing that worried him was the house."

"I don't understand."

"He was paying off the mortgage, and I gathered that it would have been a very serious matter if he had fallen behind with his monthly payments."

"Who lent him the money?"

"Monsieur Saimbron and I, between us."

"Who is Monsieur Saimbron?"

"He was the bookkeeper. He's retired now. He lives alone in rooms on Quai de la Mégisserie."

"Does he have money?"

"He's very poor."

"And yet you both lent money to Monsieur Louis?"

"Yes. If we had not done so, the house would have been sold out from under them and they would have been out in the street."

"Why didn't he go to Monsieur Kaplan?"

"He knew he would get no help from him. That's the way he is. When he told us that the firm was closing down, he handed each of us an envelope containing three months' salary. Monsieur Louis didn't dare keep his share at home, because his wife would have been sure to find it."

"Did she go through his wallet?"

"I don't know. Probably she did. At any rate, I kept the money for him, and every month I would hand over the equivalent of his salary. Then when there was no more left . . ."

"I understand."

"He paid me back."

"After how long?"

"Eight or nine months. Almost a year."

"When did you next see him, after you'd lent him the money?"

"I lent him the money in February, and didn't see him again until August."

"Didn't that worry you?"

"No. I knew he'd be back eventually. And, besides, even if he had not paid me back . . ."

"Did he tell you whether he'd found another job?"

"He said he was working."

"Was that when he took to wearing brown shoes?"

"Yes. After that, he came to see me several times. He always had some little present for me and sweets for Mother."

Maybe that was why the old woman was looking so crestfallen. No doubt most of her visitors arrived armed with sweets for her, and here was Maigret empty-handed. He made a mental note to bring a box of candy if ever he had occasion to visit the shop again.

"Did he ever mention any names to you?"

"What sort of names?"

"I don't know. Employers, friends, fellow workers, perhaps."

"No."

"Did he ever refer to any particular district of Paris?"

"Only Rue de Bondy. He went back there several times. It made him feel bitter to see that they hadn't even started on the demolition work.

"'We could have stayed on another year at least,' he used to say with a sigh."

The doorbell tinkled. Léone poked her head forward, as no doubt she did many times in the course of a day, to see who was in the shop.

Maigret stood up.

"I mustn't keep you any longer."

"Come back whenever you like. You'll always be welcome."

A pregnant woman was standing beside the counter. He picked up his hat and made for the door.

"I'm much obliged to you."

He got into the car, watched by the two women, who were gazing at him over the pink and white woolens piled on the counter.

"Where to now, Chief?"

It was just eleven o'clock.

"Stop at the first bistro you come to."

"There's one next door to the shop."

Somehow, he felt shy about going in there, under Léone's watchful eye.

"We'll find one around the corner."

He wanted to phone Monsieur Kaplan and also to consult the street guide, to find Monsieur Saimbron's exact address on Quai de la Mégisserie.

While he was inside, having started the day with a Calvados, he thought he might as well have another, and drank it standing at the bar counter.

CHAPTER THREE

THE
BOILED
EGG

Maigret lunched alone at his usual corner table in the Brasserie Dauphine. This was significant, especially since nothing urgent had cropped up to prevent him from going home to lunch. As usual, there were several inspectors from the Quai having apéritifs at the bar, and they turned to look at him as he made his way to his own special table, near a window from which he could watch the Seine flow by.

Without a word, the inspectors exchanged glances, although none worked directly under him. When Maigret walked with a heavy tread, his eyes somewhat glazed and his expression, as some mistakenly supposed, ill-humored, everyone in the Police Judiciaire knew what it all signified. And even though it might make them smile, they nevertheless viewed the signs with some respect, because they always pointed to the same conclusion: sooner or later, someone, man or woman, would be persuaded to confess to his crime.

"What's the *veau Marengo* like?"

"Excellent, Monsieur Maigret."

Without realizing it, he was subjecting the waiter to a look that could not have been sterner if he had been a suspect under interrogation.

"Beer, sir?"

"No. A half bottle of claret."

He was just being perverse. If the waiter had suggested wine, he would have ordered beer.

So far, today, he had not set foot in his office. He had just come from calling on Saimbron on Quai de la Mégisserie, and the experience had left him feeling a little queasy.

As a first step, he had telephoned Monsieur Max Kaplan at his home address, only to be told that he was staying at his villa in Antibes and it was not known when he would be returning to Paris.

The entrance to the building on Quai de la Mégisserie was sandwiched between two pet shops selling birds, many of which, in their cages, were strung out along the sidewalk.

"Monsieur Saimbron?" he had inquired of the concierge.

"Top floor. You can't miss it."

He searched in vain for an elevator. There was none, so he had to climb six flights of stairs. The building was old, with dark and dingy walls. Right at the top the landing was comparatively bright, thanks to a skylight. There was a door on the left, beside which hung a thick red-and-black cord resembling the cord of a dressing gown. He pulled it. This produced an absurd little tinkle inside the apartment. Then he heard light footsteps, the door was opened, and he saw a ghostly face, narrow, pale, and bony, covered with the white bristles of several days' growth, and a pair of watering eyes.

"Monsieur Saimbron?"

"I am Monsieur Saimbron. Do please come in."

This little speech, brief as it was, brought on a fit of hoarse coughing.

"I'm sorry. It's my bronchitis."

Inside, there was a pervasive smell, stale and nauseating. Maigret could hear the hissing of a gas ring. On it was a pan of boiling water.

"I am Chief Superintendent Maigret of the Police Judiciaire."

"Yes. I've been expecting a visit from you or one of your inspectors."

On the table, which was covered with a flower-embroidered cloth such as are now found only in flea-market stalls, lay a morning paper open at the page on which Louis Thouret's death was reported in a few brief lines.

"Were you about to have lunch?"

Next to the newspaper stood a plate, a glass of water to which a drop of wine had been added, and a hunk of bread.

"There's no hurry."

"Do please go ahead, just as if I weren't here."

"My egg will be hard by this time, anyway."

All the same, the old man decided to go and get it. The hissing of the gas ceased.

"Please sit down, Chief Superintendent. I advise you to take off your coat. I am obliged to keep the place excessively warm, on account of my rusty bronchial tubes."

He must have been almost as old as Mademoiselle Léone's mother, but he had no one to take care of him. In all probability, no one ever came to see him in his rooms, the only merit of which was a view of the Seine and of the Palais de Justice and the flower market beyond.

"How long ago did you last see Monsieur Louis?"

Their conversation had lasted half an hour, partly because of the old man's frequent bouts of coughing, and partly because he was so incredibly slow eating his egg.

And what, in the end, had Maigret learned from him? Nothing that Léone or the concierge in Rue de Bondy had not already told him.

The liquidation of the firm of Kaplan et Zanin had been a tragedy for Saimbron, as well. He had not even attempted to find another job. He had saved a little money. For years and years, he had believed that it would be enough to keep him in his old age. But what with the successive devaluations of the franc, he now literally had barely enough to stave off total starvation. That boiled egg was probably his only solid food for the day.

"I'm one of the lucky ones. I have at least been able to call this place home for the last forty years."

He was a widower. He had no children and no surviving relatives.

When Louis Thouret had come to see him and asked him for a loan, he had lent the money without hesitation.

"He told me it was a matter of life and death, and I could tell that he was speaking the truth."

Mademoiselle Léone had also been only too glad to lend him money.

"He paid me back a few months later."

But had he never wondered, during those months, whether he would ever see Monsieur Louis again? If not, how would Monsieur Saimbron have managed to pay for his daily boiled egg?

"Did he come and see you often?"

"Two or three times. The first time was when he came to return the money. He brought me a present, a meerschaum pipe."

He went to get it from the drawer of a whatnot. No doubt he had to be sparing with his tobacco, as well.

"How long is it since you saw him last?"

"About three weeks. He was sitting on a bench on Boulevard Bonne-Nouvelle."

Was the old bookkeeper so much attached to the district where he had worked for so long that he returned to it from time to time by way of pilgrimage?

"Did you speak to him?"

"I sat down beside him. He offered to buy me a drink in a café nearby, but I declined. The sun was shining. We chatted and watched the world go by."

"Was he wearing light-brown shoes?"

"I didn't pay any attention to his shoes. I can't tell you, I'm afraid."

"Did he say anything about his job?"

Monsieur Saimbron shook his head. Like Mademoiselle Léone, he was reluctant to discuss it. Maigret could understand why. He was growing quite attached to Monsieur Louis, though he had never seen him except as a corpse who had met his death with a wide-eyed stare of astonishment.

"How did your meeting end?"

"Someone was hovering around the bench. I had the impression that he was trying to attract my friend's attention."

"A man?"

"Yes. A middle-aged man."

"What was he like?"

"He was the sort of person you often see sitting on a bench in that particular district. In the end, he came and sat beside us, but he didn't speak. I got up and left. When I looked back, the two of them were deep in conversation."

"Did they seem friendly?"

"They certainly weren't having an argument."

And that was that. Maigret had gone down the stairs, intending to return home for lunch, but in the end he had decided to eat at his usual table in the Brasserie Dauphine.

It was a gray day. There were no glittering flecks on the Seine. He drank another small glass of Calvados with his coffee and went to his office, where a mass of paper work awaited him. A little later, Coméliau, the Examining Magistrate on the case, phoned.

"What do you think of this Thouret business? The Public

Prosecutor took it upon himself this morning to tell me that you were working on the case. It was the usual sort of thing, a mugging or a falling out among thieves, I presume?"

Maigret merely grunted, preferring not to commit himself one way or the other.

"The family wants to know when they can have the body. I didn't want to say anything definite until I had consulted you. Have you finished with it yet?"

"Has Doctor Paul completed his examination?"

"He's just called to let me know the results. I'll have his written report by tonight. The knife punctured the left ventricle, and death was virtually instantaneous."

"Any signs of a struggle?"

"None."

"I see no reason why the family shouldn't collect the body as soon as they like. There's just one thing, though. I'd be glad if you'd arrange for the clothes to be sent over to the Forensic Laboratory."

"I'll see to that. Keep me in the picture, won't you?"

Judge Coméliau was not usually so affable. No doubt it was because the press had barely mentioned the matter and because he himself had come to the conclusion that it was just an ordinary case of mugging. He was not interested. No one was interested.

Maigret poked the fire in the stove, filled his pipe, and for the next hour or so immersed himself in his paper work, scribbling notes in the margins of some documents and signing others. Then he made a few unimportant telephone calls.

"May I come in, Chief?"

It was Santoni, dressed to the nines as usual. And, as usual, reeking of hair oil, a habit that frequently caused his colleagues to protest:

"You smell like a tart!"

Santoni was looking very pleased with himself.

"I think I'm on to something."

Maigret, evincing no emotion, looked at him with wide, troubled eyes.

"First of all, it may interest you to know that Geber et Bachelier, the firm where the Thouret girl works, is a debt-collection agency. Nothing very big. What they actually do is take over hopeless defaulters for a small consideration and then squeeze the money out of them. It isn't so much a matter of office work as of house-to-house harassment. Mademoiselle Thouret is only in her office in Rue de Rivoli in the mornings. Every afternoon she's out and around visiting the defaulters in their homes."

"I get it."

"They're little people, mostly, because they are the ones most likely to be intimidated and to pay up in the end. I didn't see either of the partners. I waited outside until the staff came out at lunchtime. I took good care to avoid being seen by the young lady, and spoke to one of the other employees, a woman past her first youth, who, as it turned out, had no very warm feelings toward her colleague."

"And what did you find out?"

"That our little Monique has a boyfriend."

"Do you know his name?"

"All in good time, Chief. They've known each other for about four months, and they meet every day for lunch at the same restaurant on Boulevard Sébastopol. He's very young, only nineteen, and has a job as a salesman in a big bookshop on Boulevard Saint-Michel."

Maigret was fiddling with the row of pipes strung out on his desk; then, although the one he was smoking was still lighted, he started to fill another.

"The kid's name is Albert Jorisse. I thought I might as well take a look at him, so I went along to the restaurant. You never saw such a crowd! Finally I managed to spot Monique, sitting at a table, but she was by herself. I sat at a table on the opposite side of the room and had a very nasty meal. The young lady seemed very much on edge and never stopped glancing toward the door."

"Did he arrive eventually?"

"No. She made her food last as long as she could. In a place like that, the meals are served as fast as possible, and dawdling is frowned on. In the end, she had no choice but to get up and go, but she hung around outside, pacing up and down, for nearly a quarter of an hour."

"What happened next?"

"She was so concerned about the young man that she didn't notice me. Next she made for Boulevard Saint-Michel. I followed her. You know that big corner bookshop, where they have trays of books strung out all along the sidewalk?"

"Yes, I know the one you mean."

"Well, she went in there and spoke to one of the salesmen, who referred her to the cashier. I could see that she was being quite persistent, but to no avail. In the end, looking very crestfallen, she left."

"Didn't you follow her?"

"I thought I'd do better to concentrate on the young man, so, in my turn, I went into the bookshop and asked the manager whether he knew anyone named Albert Jorisse. He said yes, he worked in the shop, but only in the mornings. When I expressed surprise, he explained that it was a common practice with them, since most of the employees were students who were unable to work full time."

"Is Jorisse a student?"

"Give me a chance! I wanted to know how long he'd been working there. The manager had to consult his records. He's been with the firm for just over a year. At the beginning, he worked full time. Then, after he'd been there for about three months, he said he was going to work for a law degree and from then on could only come in in the mornings."

"Do you know his address?"

"He lives with his parents in Avenue de Chântillon, almost opposite the church of Montrouge. But that's not all. Albert Jorisse didn't turn up at the shop today. It's not the first time. It happens two or three times a year, but up to now he's always telephoned to let them know. Today he didn't."

"Was he there yesterday?"

"Yes. I thought you'd be interested, so I took a taxi to Avenue de Châtillon. His parents are thoroughly respectable people. They have an apartment on the third floor. It's spotlessly clean. His mother takes in ironing."

"Did you tell her you were a police officer?"

"No. I said her son was a friend of mine and I needed to see him urgently."

"Did she suggest you go to the bookshop?"

"Exactly. She doesn't know a thing. He left home this morning at a quarter past eight as usual. She's never heard a word about this law degree project. Her husband works for a wholesaler in fabrics in Rue de la Victoire. They couldn't afford to pay for a higher eduation for their son."

"What did you do next?"

"I pretended I thought I was on the wrong tack and that her son probably wasn't the Jorisse I was looking for. I asked her whether she had a photograph of her son. She took me to look at the one on the buffet in the dining room. She's a good soul, and she doesn't suspect a thing. All she ever thinks about is reheating her iron and making sure she doesn't scorch the linen. I stayed on for a while, talking sweet nothings . . ."

Maigret made no comment, but he listened with a marked

lack of enthusiasm. It was plain to see that Santoni had not been working under him for long. Everything he said was out of tune with the way Maigret's mind, and, indeed, the minds of his closest associates, worked.

"On the way out, taking care not to let her see what I was doing . . ."

Maigret held out his hand.

"Give it here."

As if he didn't know that Santoni had pinched the photograph! It showed a thin youth with a nervous expression and very long hair, the sort whom women often find attractive, and who know it.

"Is that all?"

"We'll have to wait and see whether he goes home tonight, won't we?"

Maigret sighed:

"Yes, we'll have to wait and see."

"Anything the matter?"

"Of course not."

What was the use? Santoni would learn in time, as others had learned before him. It was always the same when they took on an inspector from some other branch of the service.

"The reason I didn't follow the girl was that I know where to find her. Every evening at about half past five, or a quarter to six at the latest, she calls in at the office to hand over the money she has collected and write her report. Do you want me to go over there?"

Maigret hesitated on the brink of telling him to drop the whole thing. But he thought better of it. It would have been unfair. After all, according to his lights the Inspector had done his best.

"Just check that she does go back to the office as usual, and then make sure she goes to catch her train."

"Maybe her boyfriend will be waiting for her there?"

"Maybe. What time does he usually get home in the evening?"

"They have dinner at seven. He's always in by then, even if he has to go out again later."

"They don't have a telephone, I suppose?"

"No."

"What about the concierge?"

"I don't think she does either. It's not the sort of place where you'd expect to find telephones. I'll check it, though."

He consulted the street directory.

"You'd better go back there sometime after seven and see what you can find out from the concierge. Leave the photograph with me."

Santoni had taken the photograph, there was no getting around it, Maigret thought. So he might as well keep it. It could come in handy.

"Will you be here in your office?"

"I don't know where I will be, but keep in touch with our people here."

"What shall I do between now and then? I've got nearly two hours to kill before leaving for Rue de Rivoli."

"Go down and have a word with the licensed-premises department. They may have a registration form in the name of Louis Thouret."

"You mean you think he took a room somewhere in town?"

"Where do you suppose he left his brown shoes and colorful tie when he went home?"

"That's a thought."

It was now a full two hours since Monsieur Louis's photograph had appeared in the afternoon editions of the newspapers. It was only a small photograph, tucked away in a corner, and the caption read:

Louis Thouret, murdered yesterday afternoon in an alley off Boulevard Saint-Martin. The police are on the track of the killer.

It wasn't true, but that was what the papers invariably said. It was odd, come to think of it, that the Chief Superintendent had not yet received a single telephone call about the case. If the truth were told, it was chiefly because of this possibility that he had decided to return to the office and, while he was at it, clear his In-box.

Almost always, in a case of this sort, there were people who believed, rightly or wrongly, that they recognized the victim. Or they claimed to have seen an unsavory-looking character lurking near the scene of the crime. More often than not, such claims were unfounded. All the same, every now and again one or more of these people would lead him to the truth.

For the past three years, Monsieur Louis, as he was known to his former colleagues and to the concierge in Rue de Bondy, had left Juvisy at the same time every morning. Morning or evening, he never missed his usual train. He continued to take his lunch with him, wrapped in a square of waxed paper, as he had always done.

But how had he spent his time after he got off the train at the Gare de Lyon? That was still a mystery.

Except, that is, for the first few months, when, in all probability, he had spent every moment desperately looking for another job. Like so many others, he must have joined the lines outside the offices of one of the newspapers waiting to pounce on the help-wanted columns. Maybe he had even tried his hand at selling vacuum cleaners from door to door?

Apparently he had not succeeded, since he had been driven to borrow money from Mademoiselle Léone and the old bookkeeper.

After that, for several months he had disappeared from

view. By now he somehow had not only to lay his hands on a sum of money equivalent to his salary at Kaplan's, but also to pay back the two loans.

During all that time he had returned home every evening just as if nothing had happened and looking every inch the family breadwinner.

His wife had suspected nothing. Nor had his daughter, nor his sisters-in-law, nor his two brothers-in-law, who both worked for the railroad.

And then one day he had turned up at Rue de Clignancourt to pay his debt to Mademoiselle Léone, armed with a present for her and sweets for her aged mother.

Not to mention the fact that he had taken to wearing light-brown shoes!

Did those brown shoes of his have anything to do with the keen interest that Maigret was beginning to take in the fellow? He would certainly never admit it, even to himself. He, too, had longed at one time to own a pair of goose-dung shoes. They had been all the rage then, like those very short fawn-colored raincoats, known at the time as bum-freezers.

Once, early in his married life, he had made up his mind to buy a pair of light-brown shoes and had felt himself blushing as he went into the shop. Come to think of it, the shop had been on Boulevard Saint-Martin, just opposite the Théâtre de l'Ambigu. He had not dared to put the shoes on at first. Then, when he had finally plucked up the courage to open the package in the presence of his wife, she had looked at him and then laughed in a rather odd way.

"You surely don't intend to wear those things?"

He never had worn them. It was she who had taken them back to the shop, on the pretext that they pinched his feet.

Louis Thouret had also bought a pair of light-brown shoes, and that, in Maigret's view, was symbolic.

It was above all, Maigret was convinced, a symbol of liberation. Whenever he wore those shoes he must have thought of himself as a free man, which meant that until the moment he changed back into his black shoes his wife, sisters-in-law, and brothers-in-law had no hold on him.

The shoes meant something else, as well. On the day when Maigret had bought his pair, he had just been informed by the Superintendent of the Saint-Georges District, whose subordinate he was at the time, that he was to have a raise in salary of ten francs a month. And in those days ten francs really were ten francs.

Monsieur Louis, too, must have been feeling weighed down with riches. He had presented a meerschaum pipe to the old bookkeeper and repaid the two people who had been prepared to trust him. As a result, he had been able to go back from time to time and see them both, especially Mademoiselle Léone. And likewise he had felt free to call on the concierge in Rue de Bondy.

Why had he never told any of them how he spent his time?

Quite by chance, the concierge had seen him one morning around eleven sitting on a bench in Boulevard Saint-Martin.

She had not spoken to him, but had gone the long way round so that he wouldn't see her. Maigret could understand that. It was the bench that had ruffled her. For a man like Monsieur Louis, who had worked ten hours a day for most of his life, to be caught idling on a park bench! Not on a Sunday. Not after working hours. At eleven in the morning, when there was always a bustle of activity in every shop and every office.

Monsieur Saimbron had also recently spotted his former colleague sitting on a bench. In his case, on Boulevard Bonne-Nouvelle, within easy walking distance of Boulevard Saint-Martin and Rue de Bondy.

This had been in the afternoon, and Monsieur Saimbron, showing less delicacy than the concierge, had spoken to him. Or perhaps Louis Thouret had seen him first?

Had the former warehouse foreman been there by appointment? Who was the man who had hovered near the bench, apparently waiting for an invitation to sit down?

Monsieur Saimbron had not described him. Probably he had not paid much attention to him. All the same, his comment had been illuminating:

"He was the sort of person you often see sitting on a bench in that particular district."

In other words, one of those individuals without any visible means of support who spend hours sitting on benches on the boulevards absently watching the world go by. The occupants of the benches in the Saint-Martin district were different from those to be seen in many of the squares and public gardens of the city, such as the Parc Montsouris, which was mostly patronized by local residents with private means.

People of that sort were not to be found sitting on Boulevard Saint-Martin, or, if they were, it was on the terrace of a café.

There were the light-brown shoes, on the one hand, and the bench, on the other. As far as the Chief Superintendent was concerned, they did not seem to fit together.

Finally, there was the overriding fact that at about half past four on a wet and gloomy afternoon Monsieur Louis, for no apparent reason, had turned into an alley, followed soundlessly by someone who had knifed him between the shoulder blades, barely ten yards from the milling throng of people on the boulevard.

His photograph had appeared in all the papers, and no one had telephoned. Maigret was still making notes on documents and signing official forms. Outside, the dusk was deepening and would soon turn to darkness. He had to switch on the light, and when he saw that the hands of the mantel clock stood at three, he got up and took his heavy winter overcoat down from its hook.

Before leaving, he put his head in the door of the inspectors' duty room.

"I'll be back in an hour or two."

There was no point in using a car. At the end of the Quai he jumped onto the platform of a bus, from which he alighted a few minutes later at the junction of Boulevard Sébastopol and the Grands Boulevards.

At this same hour on the previous day, Louis Thouret had still been alive. He, too, had roamed around the district, with plenty of time to spare before having to change back into his black shoes and make his way to the Gare de Lyon to catch his train to Juvisy.

The pavements were jammed with people. On every corner they were bunched together like grapes, waiting to cross the road, and when the traffic light changed they all surged forward.

That must be the bench, he thought, noticing one on the sidewalk opposite him, in Boulevard Bonne-Nouvelle.

It was unoccupied, but even at this distance he could see a piece of crumpled, greasy paper that, he would have sworn, had recently contained ham or slices of pork sausage.

Prostitutes were to be seen loitering on the corner of Rue Saint-Martin. There were more of them in one of the little bars, and at a round table four men could be seen playing cards.

A familiar figure was standing at the bar counter. It was Inspector Neveu. Maigret stopped to wait for him, and one of the women thought that he was interested in her. Absently, he shook his head.

If Neveu was here, it meant that he had already questioned them. This was home ground to him, and he knew them all.

"Everything all right?" Maigret asked Neveu when he came out of the bistro.

"So you're here, too?"

"Just looking around."

"I've been wandering around here since eight this morning. If I've questioned one person, I must have questioned five hundred."

"Have you found out where he used to go for lunch?"

"How did you guess?"

"I felt sure he must have eaten his midday meal somewhere in this district, and his sort would be likely always to go back to the same place."

"Over there," said Neveu, pointing to what looked like a quiet little restaurant. "He even had his own napkin and ring."

"What did they tell you?"

"He always sat at the same table, at the back, near the bar. I got that from the waitress who always served him. She's tall and dark, with a face like a horse and hairs on her chin. Do you know what she called him?"

How could the Chief Superintendent be expected to know?

"Her little man. She told me so herself:

"*Well, little man, what do you fancy today?*'

"She says he was always cheerful. Rain or shine, he never failed to mention the weather. He never attempted to get fresh with her.

"All the waitresses in the restaurant get two hours off between clearing away the lunch and setting the tables for dinner.

"Apparently, several times, on her way out at about three o'clock, she saw Monsieur Louis sitting on a bench. Each time he waved to her.

"One day she said, to tease him:

" *'You take things easy, little man, I must say!'*

"He replied that he worked at night."

"Did she believe him?"

"Yes. She seemed to have quite a crush on him."

"Has she seen the papers?"

"No. The first she'd heard of his death was from me. She didn't want to believe it.

"It's not an expensive restaurant, but it isn't one of those fixed-price places either. Every lunchtime Monsieur Louis would treat himself to a half bottle of good wine."

"Did you find anyone else who had seen him around?"

"About ten people so far. One of the girls whose beat is over there on the corner saw him almost every day. She accosted him the first time, but he said no, very kindly. No getting on his high horse for him, and after that she got into the habit of calling out, every time she saw him:

" *'Well, is it to be today, then?'*

"It was just a little game they played. Whenever she hooked a client, he would give her a broad wink."

"Did he ever go with any of them?"

"No."

"Did any of them ever see him with a woman?"

"Not them. One of the salesmen in the jeweler's did, though."

"The one next to the place where he was killed?"

"Yes. I showed the photograph to all the staff, but he was the only one who recognized him.

" *'That's the man who came in and bought a ring last week!'* he exclaimed."

"Did Monsieur Louis have a young woman with him?"

"She wasn't particularly young. The salesman hardly noticed her. He thought they were husband and wife. What he did notice, though, was that she was wearing a silver-fox fur draped around her shoulders and a chain with a pendant in the shape of a four-leaf clover.

"'We sell pendants just like it!'"

"Was the ring valuable?"

"A paste diamond in a gold-plated setting."

"Did they say anything of interest in his presence?"

"They talked like any other married couple. He can't remember their exact words. Nothing that mattered, anyway."

"Had he ever seen her before?"

"He wasn't sure. She was dressed in black and wearing gloves. She nearly left them behind on the counter, having taken them off to try on the ring. It was Monsieur Louis who came back for them. She waited outside. She was taller than he was. When he went out, he took her arm and they went off in the direction of Place de la République."

"Nothing else?"

"These things take time. I began my inquiries higher up the boulevard, near where it joins Rue Montmartre, but I drew a blank there. Oh, I nearly forgot! You know those waffle stalls in Rue de la Lune?"

The waffles were toasted in open-fronted booths, almost completely exposed to the elements, as at a fair, and the sweetish smell of them cooking hit the nose as soon as anyone turned into the street.

"They remember him. He often bought waffles there, always three at a time. He didn't eat them then and there, but took them away with him."

The waffles were enormous. They were advertised as the largest in Paris. It was unlikely that little Monsieur Louis, having eaten a substantial lunch, could have managed to put away three of them all by himself.

Nor was he the sort of man who would sit munching on a bench. Had he shared them with the woman for whom he had bought the ring? In that case, she must live somewhere nearby.

On the other hand, the waffles could have been intended for the man seen by Monsieur Saimbron.

"Am I to carry on?"

"Of course."

Maigret felt a pang. He wished he could do the job himself, as he used to do when he was only an inspector.

"Where are you going, Chief?"

"I'm going over there, to have another look."

He didn't suppose it would do any good. It was just that the alleyway where Monsieur Louis had been killed was barely a hundred yards away, and he had an itch to return to the spot. It was practically the same time of day. Today there was no fog, but all the same it was pitch-dark in the little passage, and being dazzled by the harsh lights in the jeweler's window didn't help.

The waffles had reminded Maigret of fairs he had been to in the past, and because of this he had had the idea that Thouret might have gone into the alley to relieve himself. But this notion was soon dispelled by the sight of a urinal just across the street.

"If only I could find that woman!" sighed Neveu, whose feet must have been aching, after all the walking he had had to do.

Maigret, for his part, was more anxious to find the man who, in response to a silent signal, had come and sat beside Monsieur Louis and the old bookkeeper while they were still in conversation. That was why his searching glance rested on every bench they passed. On one of them sat an old man, a vagrant, with a half-empty liter bottle of red wine next to him. But he was not the one. If the man had been a tramp, Monsieur Saimbron would have said so.

A little farther along a fat woman from the provinces was sitting waiting for her husband to come out of the urinal, no doubt glad of the chance to rest her swollen feet.

"If I were you, I'd concentrate less on the shops and more on the people on the benches."

At the start of his career, he had spent enough time pounding the beat to know that every bench has its regulars, who are always to be found there at certain times of the day.

These people are ignored by passers-by, who seldom so much as glance at them. But the occupants of the various benches are known to each other. After all, had it not been due to Madame Maigret's getting into a conversation with the mother of a little boy while sitting on a bench in the gardens of Place d'Anvers awaiting her dental appointment that a murderer had been tracked down?

"You mean you want them rounded up?"

"Anything but! I just want you to sit down beside them and get into conversation."

"Very well, Chief," said Neveu with a sigh, not overjoyed at the prospect. Even walking the streets seemed preferable.

He never dreamed that the Chief Superintendent would have leaped at the chance of taking his place.

CHAPTER FOUR

A
FUNERAL
IN THE RAIN

☐ The next day, Wednesday, Maigret had to be in court to give evidence, and he wasted most of the afternoon kicking his heels in the dingy room reserved for witnesses. No one had thought to turn up the central heating, and everyone was shivering. When at last someone did turn it up, the room became stiflingly hot within ten minutes, and there was a pervasive smell of unwashed bodies and clothes that had never been properly aired.

The name of the man on trial was René Lecoeur. Seven months earlier he had battered his aunt to death with a bottle. He was only twenty-two, as broad-shouldered as a coal heaver, with the face of a naughty schoolboy.

Why on earth couldn't they use stronger lighting in the Palais de Justice, considering how the dark-gray paint, the dust, and the shadows soaked up all the natural light?

Maigret left the witnesses' waiting room feeling depressed. A young lawyer who was just beginning to get himself talked about, chiefly on account of his aggressive manner, was fiercely hectoring the witnesses as they followed one another into the box.

The line he took with Maigret was that the accused would never have confessed but for the rough treatment to which he had been subjected at Quai des Orfèvres. Which was an out-and-out lie. And not only was it a lie, but the lawyer knew perfectly well that it was.

"Will the witness kindly tell the court how long my client was subjected to interrogation on the first occasion?"

The Chief Superintendent had been expecting this.

"Seventeen hours."

"And during all that time he had nothing to eat?"

"Lecoeur was offered sandwiches, but he refused."

The lawyer turned an eloquent glance on the jury, as if to say:

You see, gentlemen! Seventeen hours without a morsel of food.

And what of Maigret himself? The whole time he had eaten nothing but a couple of sandwiches. And he hadn't killed anyone!

"Does the witness deny that on the seventh of March, at three o'clock in the morning, he struck the accused without provocation, in spite of the fact that the poor young man was handcuffed?"

"I do deny it."

"Is the witness denying that he ever struck the accused?"

"I did slap his face at one point, but lightly, as I might have slapped my own daughter."

The lawyer was going about it the wrong way. But all he cared about was impressing those present in court and getting himself written up in the papers.

This time, contrary to accepted practice, he addressed himself directly to Maigret, adopting a tone of voice that was at once honeyed and biting.

"Have you a daughter, Chief Superintendent?"

"No."

"Have you ever had children? . . . Speak up, please . . . I can't hear you."

The Chief Superintendent was obliged to repeat audibly that he had had a little girl who had died at birth.

And that was the end of it. He left the witness box, went to have a drink in the Palais de Justice bar, and then returned to his office. Lucas, who had been working solidly on another case for the past two weeks, was now free to turn his attention to the Thouret murder.

"Any news of young Jorisse?"

"Nothing so far."

Monique Thouret's boyfriend had not returned home the previous night, nor had he put in an appearance at the bookshop this morning, and he had not turned up for lunch at the inexpensive restaurant in Boulevard Sébastopol where he had been in the habit of meeting the girl.

It was Lucas who was in charge of the search. He was checking regularly with all the railroad stations, police stations, and border posts.

As for Janvier, he and four of his colleagues were still combing the hardware shops, hoping to track down the man who had sold the knife to the murderer.

"Any word from Neveu?"

Maigret had been expected back in his office long before this.

"He called half an hour ago. He said he'd try again at six."

Maigret was feeling a little weary. He was haunted by the memory of René Lecoeur sitting in the dock. And also by the voice of the lawyer, the judges as still as statues, the crowds of people in the dimly lighted courtroom with its dark oak paneling. It was no longer any concern of his. Once a suspect left Police Headquarters to be handed over to the examining magistrate, the Chief Superintendent's responsibility was ended. He was not always happy at the way things were done from then on. He could never be quite sure what would happen next. And if it had been left to him . . .

"Nothing from Lapointe?"

By now each of his men had been assigned to a specific task. Young Lapointe's was to go from one rooming house to another, in an ever widening circle outward from Boulevard Saint-Martin. Monsieur Louis must have taken a room somewhere, if only in order to have a place to change his shoes. He had rented the room either in his own name or in the name of someone else, such as the woman with the fox fur, toward whom he had behaved as if she were his wife and for whom he had bought a ring. As for Santoni, he was still on Monique's tail, in the hope that Albert Jorisse would try to get in touch with her, either in person or by sending a message.

The family had claimed Thouret's body the previous day. An undertaker's van had collected it. The funeral was to take place next day.

There were more documents to be signed; the paper work never seemed to end. A number of telephone calls were put through to him, none of them of any interest. It was odd that not a single person had telephoned, written, or called in person on the subject of Monsieur Louis. It was almost as if he had vanished leaving no trace behind.

"Hello. Maigret speaking."

It was Inspector Neveu, calling from a bistro. Maigret could hear music in the background, coming from a radio, no doubt.

"There's still nothing very positive to go on, Chief. I've found three more people, one of them an old woman, who spend a great deal of their time sitting on benches in the boulevards. They all remember him, and they all say the same thing: he was very likable, always polite, and never slow to enter into conversation. According to the old woman, when he left her he always made toward Place de la République, but she would soon lose sight of him in the crowd."

"Wasn't he ever with anyone else when she saw him?"

"No. But one of the others, a tramp, said to me:

" '*He was always waiting for someone. As soon as the man turned up, they would go off together.*'

"But he couldn't give me a description of the other man. All he could say was:

" '*There was nothing special about him. You see thousands like him every day.*' "

"Keep up the good work," said Maigret with a sigh.

He telephoned his wife to say that he would be home late, and then went down into the forecourt, got into the car, and told the driver to take him to Madame Thouret's address in Juvisy. There was a strong wind blowing. Dense clouds made the sky appear low overhead. They swirled about, as they do on the coast when a storm is brewing. The driver had difficulty in finding Rue des Peupliers. When they finally got there, not only were the kitchen lights on but also those in the bedroom, on the floor above.

The bell wasn't working. It had been disconnected as a sign of mourning. But someone had heard him arrive. The door was opened by a woman whom he had not seen before. She bore a family resemblance to Madame Thouret, but was four or five years older.

"Chief Superintendent Maigret . . ." he said.

She looked toward the kitchen and called out:

"Emilie!"

"I heard. Bring him in."

He was shown into the kitchen, the dining room having been transformed into a memorial chapel. The narrow entrance was filled with the scent of flowers and candles. A cold supper was laid out, and several people were seated at the table.

"I'm sorry to have to disturb you . . ."

"Allow me to introduce my brother-in-law Monsieur Magnin, who is a railroad inspector."

"Pleased to meet you."

Magnin was both humorless and stupid. He had a ginger moustache and an Adam's apple that bobbed up and down.

"You've already met my sister Jeanne. This is my elder sister, Céline."

There was barely room for all of them in the cramped little kitchen. Monique alone had not risen to greet him. She was subjecting the Chief Superintendent to an unwavering stare. She must have been thinking that he had come for her, to question her on the subject of Albert Jorisse, and she was frozen with terror.

"My brother-in-law Landin, Céline's husband, will be coming home on the Blue Train tonight. He'll just be in time for the funeral. Won't you sit down?"

He shook his head.

"Would you like to see him?"

She wanted him to know that they had done things in style. He followed her into the adjoining room, where Louis Thouret was laid out in his coffin. The lid had not yet been closed. Very softly, she whispered:

"He looks as if he were asleep."

Maigret went through all the proper motions, dipping a sprig of rosemary into a bowl of holy water, crossing himself, moving his lips as though in prayer, and then crossing himself again.

"He never thought about dying . . ." she said, and added: "He did so love life!"

They tiptoed out, and she shut the door behind her. The

others were waiting for Maigret to leave before returning to their meal.

"Will you be attending the funeral, Chief Superintendent?"

"I'll be there. As a matter of fact, that was what I came to see you about."

Monique still did not stir, but she was obviously relieved to hear this. Maigret did not seem to have noticed her, so she kept very still, almost as if in that way she could ward off what fate had in store for her.

"I take it you and your sisters know most of the people who will be attending the funeral? I don't, of course."

"I understand!" said Magnin, the brother-in-law, implying that great minds think alike.

And he turned to the others as if to say:

"This is going to be good!"

"All I'm asking is that if you should spot anyone there whose presence strikes you as odd, you should simply point them out to me."

"You mean you think the murderer might be there?"

"Not necessarily the murderer. I can't afford to ignore any possibility, however remote. You must remember that much of your husband's life during the past three years is still shrouded in mystery."

"Are you insinuating that he was mixed up with another woman?"

It was not only her face that had assumed a hard expression, but those of her two sisters as well.

"I'm not insinuating anything. I'm just feeling my way. If you notice anything out of the way tomorrow, just give me a sign. I will understand."

"Do you mean we should be on the lookout for any stranger?"

He nodded, and then apologized again for disturbing them. It was Magnin who saw him to the door.

"Have you anything concrete to go on yet?" he asked, man to man, in the tone of voice one adopts with the doctor just after he has seen the patient.

"No."

"Not even the tiniest glimmer of an idea?"

"None at all. Good night."

His purpose in visiting Rue des Peupliers had not been to alleviate the feeling of oppression that had weighed on him ever since he had sat waiting to be called as a witness in the Lecoeur trial. In the car, on the way back to Paris, he was occupied with random and seemingly irrelevant thoughts. He was remembering that when, at the age of twenty, he had first arrived in the capital, what had most disturbed him about it was the unremitting ferment of the great city, in which hundreds of thousands of people were all milling around apparently on private quests of their own.

In some places—one might almost call them strategic points—such as Les Halles, Place Clichy, the Bastille, and Boulevard Saint-Martin, where Monsieur Louis had met his death, the ferment was even more intense than elsewhere.

In the old days, he had been particularly struck, even, one might say, romantically stirred, by the sight of those who, discouraged and defeated, had given up the struggle and were being swept along willy-nilly by the great surging tide of humanity.

Since then he had come to know many such people, and they were no longer the ones whom he most admired, but, rather, those just one step above them on the ladder, who were clean and decent and not in the least picturesque, and who fought day in and day out to keep their heads above water and to nurture the illusion, or perhaps the faith, that they were alive and that life was worth living.

For twenty-five long years, Monsieur Louis had caught the same train every morning, sharing a compartment with the same people, his package of sandwiches tucked under his arm, and in the evening he had returned to what Maigret could not help thinking of as the House of the Three Sisters, since, although Céline and Jeanne had homes of their own several streets away, all three were ever present, shutting off the wider horizon like a stone wall.

"Back to Headquarters, Chief?"

"No. Drive me home."

That evening, as he so often did, he took Madame Maigret to a movie on Boulevard Bonne-Nouvelle. On the way there and back, with his arm through his wife's, he walked past the alley off Boulevard Saint-Martin.

"Is there something upsetting you?"

"No."

"You haven't said a word all evening."

"I wasn't aware of it."

Rain began to fall at about three or four in the morning, and in his sleep he could hear the water gurgling in the gutter. By breakfast time it was coming down in buckets, accompanied by squally winds, and the people in the street were clutching their umbrellas for fear they would be blown inside out.

"Proper All Saints' Day weather," remarked Madame Maigret.

In his recollection, however, All Saints' Day had always been overcast, windy, and cold, but not wet. Why this should be, he had no idea.

"Have you a lot to do?"

"I don't know yet."

"You'd better wear your galoshes."

He did as he was told. By the time he found a taxi his shoulders were already wet through, and when he got in the rain dripped off his hatbrim onto the floor.

"Quai des Orfèvres."

The funeral was at ten. He looked in at the Chief Commissioner's office, but did not stay for the daily briefing. He was waiting for Neveu, who would be driving him to the funeral. He was taking him on the off chance that he might recognize someone. After all, the Inspector knew an enormous number of people in the Saint-Martin district, and Maigret had high hopes for this particular line of inquiry.

"Still no news of Jorisse?" he asked Lucas.

Although he couldn't explain why, Maigret was convinced that the young man was still somewhere in Paris.

"Better make a list of all his friends, all the people he went around with during the last few years."

"I've made a start on it already."

"Good. Keep at it."

Neveu appeared in the doorway. He, too, was sopping wet. Maigret and he went off together.

"What a day for a funeral!" grumbled the Inspector. "I hope they've hired cars."

"I very much doubt it."

It was ten minutes to ten when they arrived at the house of mourning. Black curtains embroidered in silver had been hung over the door. People sheltering under their umbrellas were standing around on the unpaved walks, where the rain was soaking into the yellowish clay soil and running off in rivulets.

Some of the bystanders went into the house to pay their respects to the dead and came out looking solemn and pompous, conscious of having done their duty. There must have been about fifty people clustered around the house and more sheltering in neighboring doorways. There were also the neighbors, watching from their windows, determined to remain indoors until the last possible moment.

"Aren't you going in, Chief?"

"I was here yesterday."

"Not very cheerful in there, is it?"

Neveu, needless to say, was referring not to the funereal atmosphere of the occasion, but to the house itself. And yet there were thousands and thousands of people whose dreams were to own just such a house.

"Whatever possessed them to come and live here?"

"She wanted to be near her sisters and brothers-in-law."

They noticed several men in railroad uniforms. The house was not far from the marshaling yard. Most of the houses in the development were occupied by people connected in one way or another with the railroad.

The hearse arrived, followed at a brisk pace by a priest under an umbrella. He in turn was followed by an altar boy carrying the cross.

The wind whistled unimpeded down the street, flattening wet clothes against shivering bodies. The rain beat down on the coffin. Madame Thouret and her sisters, who were waiting in the foyer, conferred together in whispers. Maybe they should have seen to it that there were more umbrellas?

All three were dressed in deep mourning, as were the two brothers-in-law. Behind them came the girls, Monique and her three cousins.

That made seven women in all. As far as Maigret could see, the girls, like their mothers, closely resembled each other. It was a family of women, in which the men seemed uneasily aware that they were in a minority.

The horses drawing the hearse whinnied. The family closed ranks behind the hearse, followed by such neighbors and friends as considered themselves entitled to precede the others in the procession.

The remainder straggled behind in a ragged line, some

sheltering as best they could from the squally showers by hugging the curb.

'Do you see anyone you recognize?"

There was no one of the sort they were looking for. None of the women, for example, could have been the woman with the ring. True, one of them was wearing a fox fur, but the Chief Superintendent himself had seen her come out of one of the houses down the street, locking the door behind her. As for the men, it was impossible to imagine any of them sitting on a bench in Boulevard Saint-Martin.

Nevertheless, Maigret and Neveu stayed right to the end. Fortunately, there was no Mass, just a prayer so short that it was not even thought worth while to shut the church doors, with the result that the tiled floor was soon wet all over.

Twice the Chief Superintendent found himself looking straight into Monique's eyes, and each time he could sense the fear clutching at the girl's heart.

"Are we going on to the cemetery?"

"It's not far. We might as well."

They found themselves up to their ankles in mud, because the grave was in a new part of the cemetery, where the paths were nothing more than slimy tracks. Every time Madame Thouret caught Maigret's eye she looked around ostentatiously, to show that she had not forgotten his request. When he went forward, like all the others, to offer his condolences to the family as they stood at the graveside, she murmured:

"I don't see anyone who shouldn't be here."

Her nose was red because of the cold, and the rain had washed off her face powder. The four cousins also had shiny noses and cheeks.

Maigret and Neveu hung around outside the gate for a while, then went into the dingy little pub opposite, and Maigret ordered two glasses of hot toddy. They were not the only ones. A few minutes later, half the people who had attended the funeral poured into the tiny bar, stamping their feet on the tiled floor to get their circulation going.

There was a great deal of chatter, but Maigret was struck by only one remark:

"Will she get a pension?"

Her sisters certainly would, because their husbands worked for the railroad. In short, Monsieur Louis had always been the poor relation. Not only had he been a lowly warehouse foreman; he had also had no pension rights.

"How will they manage?"

"The daughter has a job. They'll take in a boarder, I daresay."

"Coming, Neveu?"

The rain dogged them all the way to Paris, where it was lashing the pavements. There were thick moustaches of muddy water on the windshields of all the cars.

"Where do you want to be dropped, Neveu?"

"There's no point in going home to change. I'll still have to wear the same wet coat. Drop me at the Quai. I'll take a taxi from there."

The corridors of Police Headquarters were covered with wet footprints, like the tiled floor of the church. Here, too, it was damp and cold. A man wearing handcuffs was sitting on a bench outside the office of the Chief Superintendent of the gaming squad.

"Anything new, Lucas?"

"Lapointe telephoned from the Brasserie de la République. He's found the room."

"The room rented by Louis?"

"So he says, although apparently the landlady is being the reverse of co-operative."

"Does he want me to call him back?"

"Either that or meet him there."

Maigret preferred the second alternative. There was nothing he disliked more than sitting in his office in wet clothes.

"Any other news?"

"Only a false alarm about the young man. They thought they'd picked him up in the waiting room of the Gare Montparnasse. It wasn't him, just some other fellow who fitted the description."

Maigret returned to the little black car, and within a few minutes he was going in the door of the brasserie in Place de la République, where he found Lapointe sitting beside the stove having a cup of coffee. Maigret ordered another hot toddy for himself.

He felt as if a good deal of the icy rain that had been falling had poured into his nostrils. He was sure he was going to get a cold. Maybe he was just going along with the old superstition that one always catches cold at a funeral.

"Where is this place?"

"Only a few yards from here. I came upon it quite by chance, because it isn't registered as a rooming house with furnished rooms for rent."

"Are you sure it's the right place?"

"You can ask the landlady yourself. I was going along Rue d'Angoulême, cutting across from one boulevard to another, when I saw a 'Room for Rent' sign in a window. It was a small house. There was no concierge. I rang the bell and asked to see the room. It was the landlady herself who opened the door to me. She's an elderly woman. She must have been a redhead in her youth, and possibly a beauty. But her hair is thin and faded now, and her body looked flabby under the sky-blue dressing gown she was wearing.

" 'Is it for yourself?' she asked, with the door still on the chain. 'Are you on your own?'

"I heard a door open on the floor above, and then I caught a glimpse of a very pretty girl leaning over the banister. She was in a dressing gown, too."

"A brothel?"

"I wouldn't go as far as that, but it wouldn't surprise me to learn that the landlady had worked in a brothel at some time, perhaps as an assistant to the madame.

"'Are you thinking of renting it by the month? Where do you work?'

"I persuaded her, finally, to show me the room, which is on the second floor. It overlooks the courtyard, and the furniture isn't too bad. A bit overstuffed for my taste, with lots o: cheap velvet and silk around, and a doll on the sofa bed. There are still lingering traces of a woman's scent.

"'Who gave you my address?'

"I nearly let it slip that I had read the sign in the window. All the time we were talking, I could see a flabby breast that seemed to be about to escape from her dressing gown any minute, and it bothered me.

"'You were recommended to me by a friend,' I said at last.

"On the off chance, I added: 'He said he lived here.'

"'What's his name?'

"'Monsieur Louis.'

"It was then that I realized she knew him. Her face changed. Even her voice sounded different.

"'Never heard of him!' she said curtly. 'Are you in the habit of coming in late?'

"She couldn't wait to get rid of me.

"'I thought my friend might be here now,' I said, playing the innocent. 'He doesn't work in the daytime, and he usually gets up late.'

"'Do you want the room or don't you?'

" 'I do want it, but . . .'

" 'The rent is payable in advance.'

"I took out my wallet, and then, as if coming on it by accident, I produced the photograph of Monsieur Louis.

" 'Would you believe it? Here's a photograph of the friend I mentioned.'

"She didn't even glance at it.

" 'I somehow don't think you and I would get along together,' she declared, making for the door.

" 'But . . .'

" 'I hope you don't mind seeing yourself out. If I don't hurry, my dinner will be spoiled.'

"I'm certain she knew him. As I went out, I saw a curtain twitch. I'd guess she was more than a little jumpy."

"Let's go!" said Maigret.

Although it was no distance, they got into the car, which drew up opposite the house. Once again the curtain twitched. The woman who came to the door was still not dressed, and no color could have been more unbecoming to her than the blue of her dressing gown.

"Who's there?"

"The Police Judiciaire."

"What do you want? I knew that young imp of Satan was going to make trouble for me," she grumbled, giving Lapointe a dirty look.

"We could talk better inside."

"Well, I'm not stopping you. I have nothing to hide."

"Why did you deny that Monsieur Louis was your roomer?"

"Because that young man had no business snooping around here."

She opened a door leading to a little sitting room. It was overheated, and there were garish cushions scattered around everywhere that were embroidered with cats, hearts, and musical notes. Since the drawn curtains were so thick as to shut out almost all the daylight, she switched on a floor lamp with a huge orange shade.

"What exactly do you want with me?"

Maigret, in his turn, showed her the photograph of Monsieur Louis, whose funeral he had attended that morning.

"He did rent a room here, didn't he?"

"Yes. I suppose you were bound to find out sooner or later."

"How long was he with you?"

"About two years. Maybe longer."

"Do you have many?"

"Roomers, you mean? This house is too big for a woman living alone. And it's not easy nowadays to find somewhere to live."

"How many?"

"Three, at the moment."

"And one room vacant?"

"Yes. The one I showed this young fellow here. I should have been more careful."

"What can you tell me about Monsieur Louis?"

"Only that he was a quiet sort of man. He never caused any trouble. And since he worked nights . . ."

"Do you know where he worked?"

"It was no concern of mine, so I never bothered to ask him. He used to leave at night and return in the morning. He didn't seem to need much sleep. I often told him he didn't get enough, but apparently it's the same with everyone who works nights."

"Did he have many visitors?"

"What exactly are you getting at?"

"You read the papers . . ."

There was a morning paper open on a table.

"I see what you mean. But first I have to be sure that you're not going to make trouble for me. I know the police and their methods."

Maigret was certain that if they looked through the vice squad records they would find a file on this woman.

"I do take in roomers, but I don't shout it from the house-tops, and I don't tell tales about them to the police. It's not a crime. All the same, if I'm going to have any trouble . . ."

"That depends on you."

"Do I have your word for that? To start with, what is your rank?"

"I am Chief Superintendent Maigret."

"Well! Now I know where I stand. It must be more serious than I thought. It's your colleagues in the vice squad who . . ."

She came out with an expression so coarse that Lapointe felt himself blushing.

"I admit I know he's been murdered. But that's all I do know."

"What did he say his name was?"

"Monsieur Louis. Just that."

"There was a woman who used to visit him, a dark woman, past her first youth."

"A fine-looking woman, not a day over forty. She was a real lady."

"Did she come often?"

"Three or four times a week."

"Do you know her name."

"I knew her only as Madame Antoinette."

"You seem to make a habit of calling people only by their first names."

"I don't pry into other people's business, if that's what you mean."

"Would she stay with him long?"

"As long as was necessary."

"The whole afternoon?"

"On two occasions, yes. Usually she didn't stay more than an hour or two."

"Did she ever come in the morning?"

"No. Well, she might have once or twice, but not often."

"Have you got her address?"

"I never asked her."

"Are all your other roomers women?"

"Yes. Monsieur Louis was the only man who . . ."

"Did he ever have relations with any of them?"

"Do you mean did he ever sleep with them? If that's what you're getting at, no, he didn't. He just didn't seem interested, that's all. If he'd wanted to . . ."

"Was he friendly with them?"

"He used to talk to them. They'd often knock on his door, to borrow a match or a cigarette or look at his newspaper."

"Is that all?"

"They chatted with him. And occasionally he'd play a two-handed game of *belote* with Lucille."

"Is Lucille up there now?"

"She's been out on the streets for the past two days. It often happens. I daresay she's found some man to shack up with. You've promised not to make trouble for me, remember? And the same applies to my roomers."

He did not remind her that he had made no promises of any kind.

"Did he ever have any other visitors?"

"There was one who stopped in two or three times quite recently asking for him."

"A young girl?"

"Yes. She never went up to his room. She just asked me to tell him she was here."

"Did she give her name?"

"Monique. She always waited out in the hall. She wouldn't even come into the sitting room."

"Did he come down?"

"The first time they talked in whispers for a few minutes, and then she left. The other times, they went out together."

"Didn't he tell you who she was?"

"He just asked me if I thought she was pretty."

"What did you say to that?"

"That she was quite sweet, as girls her age go nowadays, but that she'd be a real stunner in a few years' time."

"Who else came to see him?"

"Won't you sit down?"

"No, thanks. I'm soaking wet, and I wouldn't want to ruin your cushions."

"I like to keep everything just so, as far as possible. Wait a minute. There was someone else, a young man, but he didn't give his name. When I went up to tell Monsieur Louis that he was here, he seemed a little upset. He asked me to show him up. The young man only stayed about ten minutes."

"How long ago was that?"

"It was in the middle of August. I remember because of the heat and the flies."

"Did you ever see him again?"

"On one occasion they came into the house together. I got the impression that they'd met by chance in the street. They went upstairs, but the young man left almost at once."

"Is that all?"

"Isn't that enough for you? Now, I suppose, you'll be wanting to see his room, as well?"

"Yes."

"It's on the second floor, the room opposite the one I showed to your underling here. It looks out on the street, and we call it the green room."

"I'd be obliged if you would come with us."

She sighed, and went on sighing all the way up the stairs.

"Don't forget, you promised . . ."

He shrugged.

"And what's more, if you try any dirty tricks with me I'll tell the court that everything you say is a pack of lies."

"Have you got the key?"

On the floor below, inside a half-open door, he had seen a young woman. She had stared at them, standing there stark-naked with a bath towel in her hand.

"I have a passkey."

And, turning back, she called down the stairs:

"Don't worry, Yvette, it's not the vice squad!"

CHAPTER FIVE

THE POLICEMAN'S WIDOW

☐ All the furniture in the room must have been bought at some local auction. It was made of "solid" walnut, in a style fashionable fifty or sixty years ago, and included an enormous mirror-fronted wardrobe.

The first thing that struck Maigret as he went in was a canary in a cage on a table covered with a printed cotton cloth. As soon as he appeared, the bird began hopping about excitedly. It reminded him of Monsieur Saimbron's place on Quai de la Mégisserie, and he was convinced that the old bookkeeper's bird had been a present from Louis Thouret.

"Did the bird belong to him?"

"He brought it here about a year ago. He was cheated on it, because it doesn't sing. He was told it was a male bird, but in fact it's a female."

"Who does the housework?"

"I rent furnished rooms. I provide linens, but no service. I used to, in the old days, but I had a lot of trouble with maids. Since my roomers are nearly all women . . ."

"Did Monsieur Louis clean his own room?"

"He made his bed, cleaned the washbasin, and dusted

around. Once a week, as a special favor to him, I used to come up and do a little extra cleaning and polishing."

She remained standing in the doorway, and the Chief Superintendent found it a little disconcerting. In his eyes, this was no ordinary room. It was the place that Monsieur Louis had chosen as a retreat. In other words, his furnishings and possessions were not, as is usual, just the ordinary necessities of life, but an expression of his own personal, intimate tastes.

In the glass-fronted wardrobe there was not a single three-piece suit, but there were three pairs of light-brown shoes, lovingly polished to a high gloss, each pair with its own shoe trees. Furthermore, on the bedside table lay a pearl-gray hat, almost new, which he must have bought one day, in a fit of wild extravagance, as a protest against the atmosphere of the house in Juvisy.

"Did he ever go to the races?"

"I don't think so. He never mentioned racing."

"Did he talk to you much?"

"Sometimes, in passing, he would come into the sitting room for a chat."

"Was he generally cheerful?"

"He seemed to enjoy life."

Also by way of flouting his wife's notions of good taste he had bought himself a flowered dressing gown and a pair of scarlet leather slippers.

The room was tidy, with everything in its proper place and not a speck of dust anywhere. In a cupboard Maigret found an open bottle of port and two stemmed wineglasses. And, hanging from a hook, a raincoat.

He had not thought of that. If a rainy day should be followed by a fine evening, Monsieur Louis couldn't risk arriving home with wet clothes.

Clearly, he had spent hours reading. On the chest of

drawers stood a whole row of books in cheap editions. popular novels, cloak-and-dagger romances, and one or two detective stories. Maigret suspected that he had not cared for these, since he had not added to his store.

His armchair was placed near the window. Next to it was a little table, on which stood a woman's photograph in a mahogany frame. She was about forty, with very dark hair, and was dressed in black. She fitted the description given by the jeweler's assistant. She seemed tall, about the same height as Madame Thouret, as big-boned as she was, and almost equally lacking in suppleness. She was what the people of the neighborhood would no doubt call a fine figure of a woman.

"Is she the one who came to see him fairly regularly?"

"Yes."

In the drawer he found some other photographs, snapshots mostly, including a somewhat blurred one of Monsieur Louis himself wearing the pearl-gray hat.

Apart from two pairs of socks and several ties, there were no other personal possessions to be seen, no shirts or pants, no papers of any sort, no old letters—in other words, none of the usual clutter that tends to fill up most people's drawers.

Maigret, recalling the many occasions in his childhood when he had had something he wanted to hide from his family, picked up a chair and carried it across to the glass-fronted wardrobe. He climbed up on it to take a look at the top of the wardrobe. As in most houses, it was covered in a thick layer of dust, but in the middle, plainly to be seen, was a large, clean rectangle where something like a big envelope or a book, or perhaps a box, had recently lain.

He made no comment. The woman was watching him intently, and, just as Lapointe had described it, one of her breasts, always the same one, limp and soggy as dough, seemed to be on the point of slipping out of her dressing gown.

"Did he have a key to this room?"

The only key found on him had been the key of his house in Juvisy.

"Yes, he did, but he always left it with me when he went out."

"Is that common practice?"

"No. He said he had a habit of losing things, so he'd rather I kept it for him and gave it to him when he got in. And since he never came in during the evening or late at night . . ."

Maigret took the photograph out of its frame. Before leaving, he gave the canary some fresh drinking water and wandered around the room for a few more minutes.

"I'll be back soon, I daresay," he said.

She led him downstairs.

"I suppose I can't tempt you to have a little something to drink?"

"Do you have a telephone? I'd be obliged if you'd let me have your number. I may need to call on you for assistance again."

"It's Bastille 2251."

"What's your name?"

"Mariette. Mariette Gibon."

"Thanks."

"Is that all?"

"For the moment."

He and Lapointe almost had to swim to the car through the rain, which was still pelting down.

"Drive us to the corner," ordered Maigret.

And to Lapointe:

"You'll have to go back there. I'm afraid I left my pipe in the room upstairs."

Maigret had never left his pipe anywhere. And besides, he always carried at least two in his pockets.

"Did you do it on purpose?"

"Yes. Keep the glamorous Mariette talking for a few minutes, and then come back and join me here."

He pointed to a little bar, which also sold coal and firewood. He himself made a dash for the telephone and dialed the number of Police Headquarters.

"Put me through to Lucas, please. . . . Is that you, Lucas? I want you to make arrangements immediately to have this telephone number tapped: Bastille 2251."

Then, with nothing to do while waiting for Lapointe but to sip his liqueur at the bar counter, he took a closer look at the photograph. It surprised him that Louis should have picked a mistress who, outwardly at least, so closely resembled his wife. He wondered if there was any similarity of temperament. It was not impossible.

"Your pipe, Chief."

"Was she by any chance on the telephone when you arrived?"

"I don't know. She had two women with her."

"Including the naked girl?"

"Yes, but she had slipped on a dressing gown."

"You can go off to lunch now. I'll see you at the Quai this afternoon. I'll keep the car."

He told the driver to take him to Léone's little shop in Rue de Clignancourt. On the way, he stopped at a confectioner's to buy a box of chocolates. He hid it under his coat before crossing the street to go into the shop. He felt that the last place he should be visiting with his clothes sopping wet was a shop like this, overflowing with so many light and fragile garments. But he had no choice. Awkwardly he held out the box of chocolates, saying:

"For your mother."

"How kind of you to think of her."

Probably because of the humidity, the place was even hotter than the last time.

"Wouldn't you like to give them to her yourself?"

He preferred to remain in the shop, which had at least some slight contact with the world outside.

"I just wanted you to take a look at this photograph."

She glanced at it and said, without hesitation:

"Why, it's Madame Machère!"

This was most satisfactory. It wasn't a sensational discovery, such as the newspapers revel in. It was nothing, really, but it did prove that he had not been mistaken in his assessment of Monsieur Louis's character. He was not the sort of man to pick up a woman on the street or in a bar. The Chief Superintendent could not see him making advances to a strange woman.

"How do you know her?"

"She worked at Kaplan's. Not for very long, though. Only about six or seven months. Why did you want me to see her photograph?"

"She was a very close friend of Monsieur Louis."

"Oh!"

He would have spared her the pain if he could, but there had been no way of avoiding it.

"Didn't you suspect anything when they were both working in Rue de Bondy?"

"There was nothing to suspect, I'm sure of it. She worked with ten or fifteen other women in the packing room, depending on the time of year. She was married to a policeman. I remember her well."

"Why did she leave the job?"

"I believe she needed to have an operation."

"Thank you. Please forgive me for troubling you again."

"It's no trouble. Have you been to see Monsieur Saim-bron?"

"Yes."

"One other question. Was Monsieur Louis living with that woman?"

"He had rented a room near Place de la République. She used to visit him there."

"I'm sure that she was just a friend and that there was nothing else between them."

"You may be right."

"I could find out her address for you if the business records haven't been destroyed, but I have no idea what's become of them."

"If, as you say, she's the wife of a policeman, I shouldn't have any difficulty in tracing her. You did say the name was Machère, didn't you?"

"Yes, and if my memory serves me right, her first name was Antoinette."

"*Au revoir*, Mademoiselle Léone."

"*Au revoir*, Chief Superintendent."

He beat a hasty retreat. The old woman in the back room was showing signs of agitation, and he just couldn't face having to go in there to see her.

"The Préfecture."

"At the Quai?"

"No. The one at City Police Headquarters."

It was midday. People pouring out of shops and offices teetered on the edge of the sidewalks waiting for a chance to dash across the road to their favorite restaurants. There were groups of people sheltering in every doorway. They all looked glum but resigned. On the newsstands, all the papers were sodden.

"Wait here for me."

He found his way to the office of the personnel director and asked for information about a man by the name of Machère. A few minutes later, he learned that there had been a police constable called Machère, but that he had been killed in a scuffle in the line of duty two years before. At that time, he had been living on Avenue Daumesnil. His widow was receiving a pension. The couple had had no children.

Maigret made a note of the address. To gain time, he telephoned Lucas, which saved him from having to cross the road from one side of Boulevard du Palais to the other.

"Has she made any telephone calls?"

"Not so far."

"Hasn't she received any calls either?"

"Not for her. Someone rang asking to speak to one of the girls, name of Olga. Something to do with a fitting. We checked that the call really was from a dressmaker, one of those in Place Saint-Georges."

He would eat later. For the time being, he made do with an apéritif, which he gulped down in a bar, before returning to the little black car.

"Avenue Daumesnil."

It was some distance away, not far from the Métro. It was a very ordinary building, somewhat seedy by now, and no doubt mainly occupied by small tradespeople.

"Could you please direct me to Madame Machère's apartment?"

"Fourth floor, left-hand side."

There was an elevator, but it ascended in jerks, being inclined to stop several times between each floor. The brass bell beside the door was brightly polished and the door mat clean. He pressed the bell. He could hear footsteps coming toward him.

"One minute!" a woman called through the door.

She was probably changing from a housecoat into a dress. She wasn't the sort of woman to show herself in a dressing gown, even to the man who came to read the gas meter.

She looked at Maigret without speaking, but he could tell that she was upset.

"Please come in, Chief Superintendent."

She looked just like her photograph. The jeweler's assistant had accurately described her as being tall and heavily built, with a serene expression and a good deal of self-assurance. She had recognized Maigret. And, needless to say, she knew why he had come.

"This way . . . I was in the middle of doing my housework . . ."

In spite of that, her hair was neatly brushed, and she was wearing a dark dress with every button fastened. The floor gleamed. Next to the door were two felt pads, which she no doubt slipped under her feet whenever she came in with wet shoes.

"I'm afraid I'm leaving dirty marks all over the place."

"It doesn't matter."

The interior, though older and better kept, was very similar to that of the house in Juvisy. There were the same kinds of ornaments on the furniture, and on a chest stood a framed photograph of a police constable, with a medal attached to it.

Maigret had no wish to embarrass her or to take her by surprise. Anyway, there was no question of surprise. He said simply:

"I've come to talk to you about Louis."

"I've been expecting you."

Although she looked sad, there were no tears in her eyes. She was preserving a decent composure.

"Please sit down."

"I'm afraid I'll get your chair covers all wet. You and Louis Thouret were very good friends, were you not?"

"He was fond of me."

"No more than that?"

"It could have been that he loved me. He'd never been happy at home."

"Did your relationship begin when you were both working in Rue de Bondy?"

"Aren't you forgetting that my husband was still alive at that time?"

"Was Louis particularly attentive to you?"

"He never treated me any differently from the other women in the packing department."

"So it wasn't until later, after the firm of Kaplan et Zanin had gone out of business, that you really got to know each other?"

"It was eight or nine months after my husband's death."

"Did you meet again just by chance?"

"You know as well as I do that a widow's pension isn't enough to live on. I had to find work. Even when my husband was alive, I took a job every now and then. That's how I came to be working at Kaplan's. But I never worked full time. Anyway, one of my neighbors introduced me to the personnel man at the Châtelet, and I was taken on to show people to their seats."

"Is that where . . . ?"

"Yes. It was a matinee. The film was *Around the World in Eighty Days*, I remember. I was showing Monsieur Louis to his seat when I suddenly realized who he was. He recognized me, too. And that was all there was to it. But he came back to the theater often, always for a matinee, and he got into the habit of looking for me. This went on for quite some time, because, except for Sundays, there were only two matinees a week. Then one day, after the show, he invited me to have an apéritif with him, and I accepted. We ate a hurried snack together, because I had to get back in time for the evening performance."

"Had he, at that time, already taken the room in Rue d'Angoulême?"

"I imagine so."

"Did he tell you that he had no job?"

"He didn't say that, just that he was free in the afternoon."

"Did you ever find out what he did for a living?"

"No. I didn't feel it was my place to ask."

"Did he talk much about his wife and daughter?"

"A great deal."

"What did he say?"

"It's not the sort of thing a person cares to repeat, you know. When a man is unhappy in his home life and confides in someone . . ."

"Was he unhappy at home?"

"They treated him like dirt, because of his brothers-in-law."

"I don't quite understand."

Maigret understood perfectly well, and had for some time, but he wanted to encourage her to talk.

"They both had very good jobs, with free travel for themselves and their families thrown in . . ."

"And pensions at the end of it?"

"Yes. They despised Louis for his lack of ambition and his willingness to spend the rest of his life as a miserable warehouse foreman."

"When he took you out, where did you go?"

"Almost always to the same little café in Rue Saint-Antoine. We used to stay there for hours, just chatting."

"Do you like waffles?"

She blushed.

"How did you guess?"

"He used to buy them for you in Rue de la Lune."

"That was much later, when . . ."

"When you began visiting him in Rue d'Angoulême?"

"Yes. He wanted me to see the place where he spent so much of his time. He called it his den. He was very proud of it."

"Did he ever tell you what made him decide to take a room in town?"

"Just so he could have somewhere he could call his own, if only for a few hours a day."

"Did you become lovers eventually?"

"I often went to his room."

"Did he ever buy you jewelry?"

"Just a pair of drop earrings, about six months ago, and more recently a ring."

She was wearing it.

"He was too kind, too sensitive. He needed cheering up. Whatever you may think, I was first and foremost his friend, the only friend he had."

"Did he ever come and see you here?"

"Never! It wouldn't have done, on account of the concierge and the neighbors. It would have been the talk of the district in no time."

"Did you see him on Monday?"

"I was with him for about an hour."

"What time of day was that?"

"Early afternoon. I was out shopping."

"Did you know where to find him?"

"We had arranged to meet."

"On the telephone?"

"No. I never telephoned him. We fixed it up when I was with him the time before."

"Where did you used to meet?"

"Nearly always at our usual little café. Sometimes on the corner at the junction of Rue Saint-Martin and the Boulevards."

"Was he on time?"

"He was never late. On Monday it was cold and foggy. I have a sensitive throat. We went to a newsreel theater."

"On Boulevard Bonne-Nouvelle?"

"How did you know?"

"What time did you leave him?"

"Around four. Half an hour or so before he died, according to the newspapers."

"Did you know if he was going to meet someone?"

"He said nothing about it to me."

"Did he never mention any friends, people he went around with?"

She shook her head. Looking toward the glass-fronted cabinet in the dining room, she said:

"Would you care for a drink? I only have a little vermouth. I gave up drinking myself a long time ago."

To please her, he accepted. There was a thick sediment on the bottom of the bottle, which no doubt had been there since the late police constable's time.

"When I read about it in the paper, I almost went to see you. I'd heard a lot about you from my husband. I recognized you at once just now, because I've often seen photographs of you in the papers."

"Did Louis ever consider getting a divorce and marrying you?"

"He was too scared of his wife."

"And his daughter?"

"He was very fond of his daughter. There was nothing he wouldn't have done for her. All the same, I had the feeling that he was a little disappointed in her."

"Why?"

"It was no more than an impression. He often seemed sad."

She wasn't all that cheerful herself, with her monotonous, uninflected voice. He wondered if she was the one who had polished the furniture for him in the course of her visits to Rue d'Angoulême.

He couldn't imagine her undressing in Louis's presence and stretching out on the bed. He couldn't even imagine her naked or wearing just a bra and panties. To his way of thinking, they must have been most at home together sitting at a table in a dark corner of their little café, as she called it, talking in undertones and glancing from time to time at the clock over the bar.

"Did he spend money freely?"

"It depends what you mean by freely. He didn't stint himself. You had the feeling that he was comfortably off. If I had let him, he would have loaded me with presents, mostly the sort of useless fripperies you see in gift shops."

"Did you ever come across him sitting on a bench?"

"On a bench?" she repeated, as though the question somehow troubled her.

She hesitated.

"Once, when I was shopping in the morning. He was in conversation with a man, a thin man. I felt that there was something odd about him."

"In what way?"

"He reminded me, I don't quite know why, of a clown or a comic without the make-up. I didn't really see his face, but

I noticed that his shoes were worn and the bottoms of his trousers frayed."

"Did you ask Louis about him?"

"Yes. He said you come across all sorts of people sitting on benches, and he enjoyed talking to them."

"And that's all you know? By the way, I'm surprised you didn't go to the funeral."

"I didn't dare show my face. In a day or two I will go and put some flowers on his grave. I suppose there will be someone to show me where it is? Will the newspapers have to be told about me?"

"Certainly not."

"That's a great relief. They're very strait-laced at the Châtelet, and they wouldn't hesitate to fire me."

It wasn't very far to Boulevard Richard-Lenoir, so after he had left the widow he got the driver to drop him at home, and said:

"You'd better go and get some lunch. Come back here for me in about an hour."

During lunch, his wife watched him more closely than was her wont.

Finally she plucked up the courage to ask:

"What's the matter?"

"What should be the matter?"

"I don't know. You don't seem like yourself, but like someone quite different."

"Who, for instance?"

"It might be anyone. But it's certainly not Maigret."

He laughed. He had been thinking so much about Louis that he had begun to behave the way he imagined Louis would have behaved, even to the extent of aping what he supposed were his facial expressions and mannerisms.

"I hope you're going to change your suit?"

"What's the use? I'll be soaking wet again in no time."

"Why? Are you going to another funeral?"

He decided to give in, and changed into the clothes she had laid out for him. It was a pleasant sensation, he had to admit, to be wearing dry things again, for however short a time.

At Quai des Orfèvres, he did not go straight to his office, but looked in on the vice squad first.

"Do you know anyone by the name of Mariette or Marie Gibon? I'd be very grateful if you'd have a look through your records."

"Is she young?"

"Fiftyish."

Without further delay, the inspector got out several boxes filled with dusty, yellowing registration forms. He did not have to look far. The Gibon girl, born in Saint-Malo, had been a licensed prostitute for eleven years. She had been referred three times to Saint-Lazare, in the days before it was closed down. She had been arrested twice for stealing from clients.

"Was she convicted?"

"She was released for lack of evidence."

"Anything since?"

"Just a second. I'll have a look through this other box."

Her name appeared again on more recent registration forms, but all were at least ten years old.

"Before the war she was the assistant manager of a massage parlor in Rue des Martyrs. At that time she was living with a man called Philippe Natali, otherwise known as Philippi, who was sentenced to ten years for murder. I remember the case. It was a gang killing. Two or three men killed a guy from a rival gang, in a tobacco shop in Rue de la Fontaine. It was never established who actually fired the shot, so they nabbed them all."

"Is he still in prison?"

"He died in Fontevrault."

That didn't help matters.

"And what became of her?"

"Don't know. She may be dead, too."

"She isn't."

"She must have had quite a bundle salted away. She's probably set up an establishment of her own in her home town."

"She rents out furnished rooms in Rue d'Angoulême. She's not registered with the licensed-premises people. Most of her tenants are girls, but I don't think they ply their trade on the premises."

"That makes sense."

"I'd like a watch kept on the house, and as much information as possible about the residents."

"That shouldn't be difficult."

"I'd prefer to have someone from the vice squad on the job. My men couldn't be sure of identifying the people involved."

"I'll see to it."

At last Maigret was able to sit down, or, rather, collapse into the armchair in his office. No sooner was he comfortably settled than Lucas put his head in the door.

"Any news?"

"Nothing on the telephone front. There have been no outgoing calls. But there was one rather odd incident this morning. A woman by the name of Madame Thévenard, who lives with her nephew in Rue Gay-Lussac, went out to attend a funeral."

"Really?"

"Not the same funeral. This took place in a local cemetery. The apartment was empty while she was out. When she got home, having done her household shopping on the way back, she went into her pantry to put her groceries away and discovered that a sausage which had been there two hours previously had disappeared."

"Is she quite sure . . . ?"

"Absolutely sure. And besides, when she had a good look around the apartment . . ."

"Wasn't she frightened?"

"She had an old service revolver in her hand. Her husband had kept it from the First World War. Apparently she's an odd sort of woman, very tiny and plump, and she never stops laughing. She says she found a handkerchief that doesn't belong to him under her nephew's bed, and a few crumbs."

"What does the nephew do?"

"He's a student, and his first name is Hubert. The Thévenards aren't all that well off, so he works in the daytime as an assistant in a bookshop on Boulevard Saint-Michel. Do you see what I'm driving at?"

"Yes. Did the aunt notify the police?"

"Yes. She telephoned the local station from the lodge. The inspector who took the call got in touch with me right away. I sent Leroy off to the bookshop to see what he could get out of Hubert. The kid was shaking all over, and then he burst into tears."

"Is he a friend of Albert Jorisse?"

"Yes, and Jorisse had pleaded with him until he agreed to hide him in his room for a few days."

"What had Jorisse said was the matter?"

"He said he'd quarreled with his parents, and that his father had a fearful temper and was quite capable of doing him serious harm."

"And so Hubert agreed to let him spend two days and two nights hidden under his bed?"

"No. He was there only twenty-four hours. He spent the

first night wandering around the streets, or so he told his friend. I've notified all the police stations. The kid must be somewhere out there in the city."

"Has he any money?"

"Hubert Thévenard couldn't say."

"Have you alerted all the railroad stations?"

"I think we've provided for everything, Chief. I'd be surprised if he wasn't brought in sometime between now and tomorrow morning."

Maigret wondered what the family in Juvisy was doing. No doubt the widow's sisters, along with their husbands and daughters, had rallied round. They had probably all dined there in the house of mourning. A substantial meal, for certain, as was only fitting after a funeral. They must have discussed Madame Thouret's future, and Monique's, as well.

Maigret could just see them, the two men lounging in the best armchairs with drinks and good cigars.

"Do have a drop of something, Emilie. It will do you good."

Had they talked of the dead man? Probably someone had remarked that in spite of the shocking weather the funeral had been well attended.

Maigret was almost tempted to go and see for himself. He was particularly anxious to have a serious talk with Monique. But not at her home. At the same time, he was reluctant to summon her officially.

Almost without thinking, he asked the operator to put him through to her office.

"Is this Geber et Bachelier?"

"Georges Bachelier speaking."

"I wonder if you are expecting Mademoiselle Thouret to be back at work tomorrow morning?"

"Certainly. She had today off to attend to family matters,

but I can't see any reason why she shouldn't—who is this speaking?"

Maigret hung up.

"Isn't Santoni back yet?"

"He hasn't been in since early this morning."

"Leave him a note, will you, telling him that I want a watch kept, starting the first thing tomorrow morning, on the entrance to Geber et Bachelier. As soon as Mademoiselle Thouret arrives, I want her brought here. Tell him to treat her gently."

"You want her brought here?"

"Yes, to my office."

"Anything else?"

"No, nothing. I'll be working in here for a while. I don't want to be disturbed."

He had had enough for one day of Louis Thouret, his family, and his mistress. If it hadn't been for his sense of duty, he would have walked straight out and gone to a movie.

He stayed until seven, plowed through a mass of paper work as if the fate of the world depended on it. Not only did he polish off everything in his pending file, but he also dealt with several files that had been kicking around for weeks, or even months, and were of no importance whatsoever.

When he finally left, his vision blurred from having spent so long poring over print and typescript, he was aware of a change. At first he couldn't think what it was. Then he held out his hand and realized that it was no longer raining. He felt an odd sense of deprivation.

CHAPTER SIX

THE
BEGGARS

☐ "What's she doing?"

"Nothing. She's sitting bolt upright, with her head held high, staring into space."

She had chosen to sit not in one of the armchairs in the waiting room, but on a hard upright chair.

Maigret had intentionally left her to stew, as he put it. When Santoni had looked in, at about twenty minutes past nine, to tell him that Monique was in the waiting room, Maigret had growled:

"Leave her in the cage for a while."

This was his name for the glass-walled waiting room, with its velvet armchairs, where so many before Monique Thouret had sat for hours, until their nerves gave way.

"How does she look?"

"She's wearing mourning."

"That's not what I meant."

"I almost had the feeling that she'd been expecting to find me there. I waited a few yards from the door of the offices in Rue de Rivoli. As soon as she arrived, I came forward to meet her, saying:

" 'Excuse me, Mademoiselle . . .'

"She screwed up her eyes and peered at me. I think she must be shortsighted. Then she said:

" 'Oh! It's you.'

" 'The Chief Superintendent would like a word with you.'

"She didn't protest. I hailed a taxi. She never opened her mouth all the way here."

Not only was it not raining, but the sun was actually shining.

The light seemed even more diffused than usual, because of the humidity in the air.

Maigret, on his way to the daily briefing, had seen her from a distance sitting in a corner of the waiting room. Half an hour later, when he passed by on his way to his office, she was still there, exactly as before. Some time after that he had sent Lucas to see what she was doing.

"Is she reading?"

"No. She's not doing anything."

From where she sat, her view of Police Headquarters was similar to the view of a restaurant as seen from the kitchen area. She could see the long corridor with its many doors and the inspectors coming and going, with files under their arms, conferring with each other in their different offices and then returning to their own desks. Occasionally they would stop·in their tracks to·discuss some current problem with a colleague, and from·time·to time one would arrive·escorting a handcuffed prisoner or a weeping woman.

Other people, who had arrived long after she did, had already been·interviewed by those whom·they had come to see, yet she still showed no signs of impatience.

The telephone in Rue d'Angoulême remained silent. Did Mariette Gibon suspect that it was being tapped?

Maybe the ruse of pretending he had forgotten his pipe had put her on her guard?

Neveu, who had by now been relieved by a local colleague, reported that he had observed nothing unusual while keeping watch on the house.

As for Albert Jorisse, it was now practically certain that he had still been in Paris at six o'clock the previous night. Police Constable Dambois, who, like everyone else, had been issued a description of him, had spotted him around that time at the junction of Place Clichy and Boulevard des Batignolles. The young man had been coming out of a bar. Had the constable perhaps been too eager in his attempt to apprehend him? At any rate, Jorisse had made a run for it and was soon lost in the crowd, which was particularly dense at that time of the evening. The constable had blown his whistle to summon help.

But, inevitably, it had been to no avail. They had combed the area, in vain. They had questioned the proprietor of the café, who told them that the young man had not used the telephone but had wolfed down five hard-boiled eggs with buttered rolls and had drunk three cups of coffee.

"He looked famished to me."

Examining Magistrate Coméliau had been in touch with Maigret.

"Any fresh news?"

"I'm hoping to be in a position to arrest the murderer within the next couple of days."

"Was it a mugging, as we thought?"

Maigret had said yes.

There was still the business of the knife to be settled. A letter had arrived in the morning mail from the firm that manufactured them. As a first step in his inquiries, Janvier had personally gone to see one of the executives in the firm, only to be told that there was no way of finding out which hardware shop had been supplied with that particular knife. With considerable pride, he had quoted to Janvier the astronomical figure representing the number of such knives made in the company's factories.

Now someone with the words "Joint Managing Director" typed under his signature had written to the Chief Commissioner to inform him that, according to the serial number on the handle, the murder weapon had formed part of a consignment of knives delivered about four months ago to a wholesaler in Marseilles.

So five inspectors had wasted three days combing the hardware shops of Paris. Janvier was hopping mad.

"What should I do next, Chief?"

"Pass the word to Marseilles. Next, get hold of Moers or someone else from the Forensic Lab, go with him to Rue d'Angoulême, and get him to fingerprint Louis Thouret's room. Tell him not to forget to give the top of the glass-fronted wardrobe a thorough going-over."

All this time Monique was still waiting. Every now and then Maigret sent someone to have another look at her.

"What's she doing?"

"Nothing."

He had seen people much tougher than she was reduced to nervous wrecks after an hour of waiting in the glass-walled cage.

By a quarter to eleven he could stand no more of it.

"Send her in," he said with a sigh.

He stood up as she came in and apologized for keeping her waiting.

"Since I am anxious for us to have a long talk, I thought it best to get my paper work out of the way first."

"I quite understand."

"Do please sit down."

She did so, smoothing down her hair on either side of her face, and rested her handbag flat on her lap. He sat down opposite her, raised a pipe to his lips, and before striking a match, said:

"Do you mind?"

"My father smoked. So do both my uncles."

She was less strung up, less uneasy, than when she had first been to see him in this same office.

"Needless to say, it's your father I want to talk about."

She nodded.

"And about you, too, and one or two other people."

She gave him no help, nor did she look away from him. She just waited, as if she knew what he was going to say.

"Are you very attached to your mother, Mademoiselle Monique?"

It had been his intention to adopt a bantering, affable approach, leading her on by degrees, until in the end she would be left with no choice but to tell him the truth. But he was disconcerted by her blunt reply.

With complete composure, as if it were the most natural thing in the world, she said:

"No."

"You mean you and she don't see eye to eye?"

"I hate her."

"May I ask why?"

She gave a little shrug.

"You've been to the house. You've seen her."

"Could you elaborate on that?"

"My mother thinks only of herself and her own social position and providing for her old age. She never stops fretting at having married less advantageously than her sisters, though she pretends to herself that she is every bit as well off as they are."

He had difficulty suppressing a smile, though she had spoken with great intensity of feeling.

"Were you fond of your father?"

She was silent for a moment. He repeated the question.

"I'm trying to think. I'm not sure. I hate having to admit it, now that he's dead."

"You mean you didn't think much of him?"

"He was pretty spineless."

"What do you mean by that?"

"He would never take a stand on things."

"What sort of thing?"

"Everything."

Then, with a sudden burst of feeling:

"You can't imagine the sort of life we led. If you can call it living. I got fed up with it long ago. Now I have only one thought in my head, to get away."

"To get married, you mean?"

"Not necessarily. I just want to get out."

"In the near future?"

"Perhaps not, but some day."

"Did you ever talk it over with your parents?"

"What good would it have done?"

"Did you intend to leave without saying a word?"

"Why not? What difference would it have made to them?"

He was watching her with growing interest, so much so that from time to time he let his pipe go out. He had to relight it several times.

"When did you discover that your father was no longer working in Rue de Bondy?" he asked bluntly.

He had thought that she would at least start in surprise,

but she didn't. She must have anticipated his line of questioning and had her answers ready. It was the only possible explanation for her attitude.

"Nearly three years ago. I can't remember the exact date. It was sometime in January, I think. January or February. It was freezing cold."

The firm of Kaplan et Zanin had closed down at the end of October. In January and February, Monsieur Louis had still been looking for another job. It was during that period that, having exhausted his reserves, he had reluctantly borrowed money from Mademoiselle Léone and the old bookkeeper.

"Did your father tell you himself?"

"No. It was simpler than that. One afternoon, when I was out on my rounds . . ."

"Were you already working in Rue de Rivoli at that time?"

"I began working for the firm when I was eighteen. It so happened that one of the people I had to see was a hairdresser with a shop in the building where my father worked. I looked out into the courtyard. It was past four o'clock. It was pitch-dark. There were no lights in the building opposite. I couldn't understand it, so I inquired of the concierge, who informed me that Kaplan's had gone out of business."

"Did you say anything to your mother when you got home?"

"No."

"Nor to your father?"

"He wouldn't have told me the truth."

"Was he a habitual liar?"

"It's hard to explain. He hated domestic quarrels, so in order to avoid them he would say and do anything to keep my mother happy."

"Was he afraid of her?"

"He just wanted to keep the peace."

She spoke with some contempt.

"Did you follow him?"

"Yes. Not the next day, because the opportunity didn't arise. It was two or three days later. I caught an earlier train than usual, saying that there was an urgent job waiting for me in the office, and I hung around near the station."

"What did he do that day?"

"He went into several offices. I got the impression that he was looking for a job. At lunchtime he went into a little bar and ate a couple of croissants, and then he rushed off to a newspaper office to read the help-wanted columns. I realized what it all meant."

"How did you feel about it?"

"What do you mean?"

"Didn't it surprise you that he had not mentioned it to either your mother or yourself?"

"No. He wouldn't have dared. It would only have led to a scene. My uncles and aunts would have taken advantage of the occasion to overwhelm him with advice and reproach him for lack of initiative. I've had that word 'initiative' dinned into me ever since I was born."

"And yet at the end of each month your father brought home his salary as usual, didn't he?"

"That really did puzzle me. As the months went by, I became more and more certain that before very long he would have no choice but to return home empty-handed. But, instead of that, he announced one day that he had 'demanded' a raise and got it."

"When was this?"

"A good while later. In the summer. Sometime in August."

"I presume you thought your father had managed to get another job?"

"Yes. I wanted to find out more, so I followed him again. But he still wasn't working. He wandered around, and every now and then he sat down on a bench. I thought perhaps it was his day off, so I waited a couple of weeks, and then, deliberately picking a different day, I followed him again. That time, he spotted me. He had just sat down on a bench on one of the Grands Boulevards. He turned very pale, hesitated, and then got up and came toward me."

"Did he know you had been following him?"

"I don't think so. He must have thought it was just a chance meeting. We went and had an espresso on the terrace of a café. It was very hot. He told me a lot of things then."

"What did he say?"

"That Kaplan's had been bought out and he had suddenly found himself out of a job. He said he had decided not to tell my mother, in order to spare her anxiety, because he had been quite sure that he would have no difficulty finding another job."

"Was he wearing brown shoes?"

"Not that day. He went on to say that it had not been as easy as he had expected, but that everything was all right now. He was selling insurance, which gave him plenty of free time."

"Why had he still said nothing at home?"

"Still on account of my mother. She despised door-to-door salesmen. It made no difference whether they were selling insurance or vacuum cleaners. She referred to them as good-for-nothings and beggars. If she had found out that her husband was one of them, she would have felt so humiliated that she would have made life unendurable for him. Especially in relation to her sisters."

"Your mother sets great store by her sisters' good opinion, doesn't she?"

"Keeping up with them is the whole aim of her life."

"Did you believe your father when he told you he was selling insurance?"

"At the time I did."

"And later?"

"I began to wonder."

"Why?"

"First of all, because he was making too much money."

"As much as all that?"

"I don't know what you mean by 'as much as all that.'
After a few months, he announced that he had been promoted
to assistant manager, at an increased salary, still at Kaplan's, of
course. I remember they had words about that. Mother wanted
him to change the entry under 'Occupation' on his identity
card. She had always felt humiliated by the title of warehouse
foreman. He said it wasn't worth the trouble, it was such a
trivial matter."

"I daresay you and your father exchanged knowing glances
at that point?"

"When he was sure my mother wasn't looking, he winked
at me. From time to time, in the morning, he would slip some
money into my bag."

"In order to buy your silence?"

"No, it pleased him to be able to give me money."

"You mentioned that you and he sometimes met for
lunch."

"That's right. He used to arrange to meet me, in whispers,
in the foyer at home. In the restaurant he'd always make me
have the most expensive dishes, and would offer to take me to
the movies afterward."

"Did you ever see him wearing brown shoes?"

"Once. It was then that I asked him where he went to
change his shoes, and he told me that for business reasons he
had had to rent a room in town."

"Did he give you the address?"

"Not at first. All this happened over a long period of time."

"Did you have a boyfriend then?"

"No."

"When did you first make the acquaintance of Albert Jorisse?"

She neither blushed nor stammered. This was another question she had been expecting.

"Four or five months ago."

"Are you in love with him?"

"We're planning to go away together."

"To get married?"

"Not until he's of age. He's only nineteen. He can't marry without his parents' consent."

"Would they refuse to give their consent?"

"I'm quite sure they would."

"Why?"

"Because he has to get ahead in the world. That's all his parents ever think of. Just like my mother."

"Where were you planning to go?"

"South America. I've already applied for a passport."

"Have you any money?"

"A little. I'm allowed to keep part of what I earn."

"When did you first ask your father to let you have the money?"

She stared at him for a moment and then said, with a sigh:

"So you know that, too."

Then, without hesitation:

"I thought you might. That's why I'm telling you the truth. I'm sure you wouldn't be such a louse as to repeat all this to my mother. Unless, of course, you and she are two of a kind!"

"I have no intention of discussing your affairs with your mother."

"Even if you did, it wouldn't make the slightest difference."

"You mean you'd go anyway?"

"In my own good time, yes."

"How did you find out your father's address?"

This time, she seemed on the point of telling a lie.

"I got it from Albert."

"How did he find out? Did he follow him?"

"Yes. We were both curious about how he earned his money. We decided that the best way to find out was for Albert to follow him."

"What business was it of yours?"

"Albert was sure that, whatever my father was up to, it was something illegal."

"And supposing it was, what was to be gained by pursuing your investigation?"

"Whatever it was, it must have been very lucrative."

"Did you intend to ask for a share of the money?"

"We expected that he would at least pay our fares."

"Blackmail, in other words."

"It's only natural for a father . . ."

"The long and the short of it is that your friend Albert set about spying on your father."

"He followed him for three days."

"What did he find out?"

"What have you found out?"

"I asked you a question."

"First, that my father had taken a room in Rue d'Angoulême. Next, that he was not connected in any way with insurance, but spent most of his time loafing around on the Grands Boulevards and sitting on benches. And finally . . ."

"Finally?"

"That he had a mistress."

"What effect did this discovery have on you?"

"I wouldn't have minded so much if she had been young and attractive. In fact, she was very much like Mother."

"Have you seen her?"

"Albert pointed out the place where they were in the habit of meeting."

"In Rue Saint-Antoine?"

"Yes. It was a little café. I strolled past, as if I were there just by chance, and looked in. I didn't have time to get a good look at her, but I could see the sort of woman she was. It couldn't have been much more fun for him being with her than with my mother."

"And then you went to see him in Rue d'Angoulême?"

"Yes."

"Did your father give you any money?"

"Yes."

"Did you use threats?"

"No. I told him I'd lost the envelope containing the money I had collected for my firm that afternoon, and that unless I made it good I'd be out on my ear. I also said that they would prosecute me for theft."

"How did he react to that?"

"He looked embarrassed. Then I noticed a photograph of a woman on the bedside table. I snatched it up and exclaimed:

" 'Who's this?' "

"What was his answer?"

"That she was just a childhood friend whom he happened to have run into again recently."

"Aren't you ashamed of yourself?"

"I was only acting in self-defense."

"Against whom?"

"Against the whole world. I am determined not to end up like my mother, slowly stifling to death in some caricature of a house."

"Did Albert go to see your father, as well?"

"I have no idea."

"My dear child, that's a plain lie."

She looked at him thoughtfully and then said:

"Yes."

"Why did you choose to lie about that in particular?"

"Because ever since I found out that my father had been murdered I have realized that Albert was in trouble."

"You know that he's disappeared?"

"He telephoned me."

"When?"

"Before he disappeared, as you put it. Two days ago."

"Did he tell you where he was going?"

"No. He was terribly upset. He was convinced that he was going to be charged with murder."

"What put that idea into his head?"

"Because he had been to Rue d'Angoulême."

"When did you find out that we were on his track?"

"After your inspector questioned that old sourpuss Mademoiselle Blanche in my office. She hates me. Afterward, she boasted that she'd said enough to make sure, as she put it, that my goose was well and truly cooked. I tried to calm Albert down. I told him that he was behaving like an idiot, because nothing was more likely to arouse the suspicions of the police than for him to go into hiding."

"But you couldn't make him see reason?"

"No. He was in such a state that he was scarcely coherent on the telephone."

"What makes you so sure he didn't kill your father?"

"What possible motive could he have had?"

Very calmly, to show that she had thought it all out, like the rational being she was, she added:

"We could have asked my father for as much money as we wanted."

"What if he had refused?"

"He couldn't have done that. Albert had only to threaten to tell my mother all he knew. I know what you're thinking. You think I'm a bitch, you almost said as much, but if you had wasted the best years of your life, as they say, in a hole like Juvisy . . ."

"Did you see your father the day he died?"

"No."

"What about Albert?"

"I'm almost sure he didn't. We hadn't planned anything for that particular day. We had lunch together, as usual, and he never mentioned my father."

"Do you know where your father kept his money? As I understand it, your mother was in the habit of going through his pockets and his wallet every evening when he got home."

"She always did."

"Why?"

"Because on one occasion, ten years ago or more, she found a handkerchief with lipstick on it. My mother doesn't use lipstick, you see."

"You must have been very young at the time."

"I was ten or twelve years old. All the same, I'll never forget it. They'd forgotten I was there. My father's story was that one of the women in the packing room had fainted, on account of the heat, and that he'd poured alcohol on his handkerchief and held it under her nose until she came around."

"He was probably telling the truth."

"My mother didn't believe him."

"To return to my question, your father couldn't come home with more money in his pocket than could be accounted for by his so-called salary."

"He kept it in his room."

"On top of the glass-fronted wardrobe?"

"How did you know?"

"How did you?"

"Once when I went to see him, to ask him for some money, he climbed up on a chair and took a buff-colored envelope from the top of the wardrobe. It was stuffed with thousand-franc notes."

"A lot?"

"A thick bundle."

"Did Albert know about it, too?"

"That's no reason for killing him. I'm certain he didn't do it. And, besides, he would never have used a knife."

"How can you be so sure?"

"I've seen him almost pass out when he pricked his finger with a penknife. The sight of blood makes him ill."

"Do you go to bed with him?"

Once again she shrugged, and then said:

"What a question!"

"Where?"

"Anywhere. There are enough hotels in Paris that exist solely for that purpose. You're surely not suggesting that the police don't know about them?"

"Be that as it may, let us return to a more interesting topic. You and Albert were blackmailing your father, intending to elope to South America as soon as you had squeezed enough money out of him?"

For all the feeling she showed, she might not have heard him.

"Furthermore, I gather that, for all your spying on him, you were not able to find out how your father got his money."

"We didn't try all that hard."

"I see. All you cared about was that he had the money, not how he made it."

Every so often Maigret had the feeling that she was looking at him with a kind of pitying indulgence. She must have been thinking that he, Chief Superintendent of the crime squad, was proving to be almost as naïve as her mother and her aunts and uncles.

"Now you know everything," she said, making as if to get up. "You'll have noticed, I hope, that I haven't pretended to be anything but what I am. As to what you may think of me, I couldn't care less."

All the same, she was uneasy about something.

"May I have your assurance that you won't say anything to my mother?"

"Why should you care? You'll be out of it soon, anyway."

"For one thing, it will take time to make all the arrangements, and, for another, I'd prefer to avoid a scene."

"I understand."

"Albert is still a minor, and his parents might . . ."

"I would very much like to have a talk with Albert."

"If it was up to me, he'd be here now. He's a fool. I can just see him, huddling out of sight somewhere, shaking from head to foot."

"You don't seem to have a very high opinion of him."

"I haven't a high opinion of anyone."

"Except yourself."

"I don't think much of myself, either. I'm only looking after my own interests."

What was the use of arguing with her?

"Did you tell my employers that I was being brought here?"

"I telephoned them and said we needed you here in connection with certain legal formalities."

"What time are they expecting me back?"

"I didn't say any particular time."

"Can I go?"

"I'm not stopping you."

"Will I still be followed around by one of your inspectors?"

He felt like laughing, but managed to keep a straight face.

"Possibly."

"He'll be wasting his time."

"Thank you for your assistance."

Maigret did, in fact, have her followed, though he was convinced that nothing would come of it. It was Janvier, who happened to be free at the moment, who took over the assignment.

As for the Chief Superintendent, he sat for ten minutes or more, with his elbows on his desk and his pipe clenched between his teeth, gazing absently at the window. In the end, he had to shake himself back to consciousness, like someone waking from a deep sleep. He got up, grumbling to himself.

"Silly little fool!"

Feeling somewhat at loose ends, he went into the inspectors' duty room.

"Still no news of the boy?"

Albert must be itching to get in touch with Monique. But how could he manage it without getting caught? There was one question that Maigret had neglected to ask. And yet it was a matter of some importance. Which of the two of them was in actual possession of the money they had amassed in order to finance their trip to South America? If it was Albert, he was probably still carrying it around in his pocket. If it was not, presumably he had barely enough to buy food.

For a few minutes more he paced restlessly between the two rooms. Then he telephoned the offices of Geber et Bachelier.

"May I speak to Mademoiselle Monique Thouret, please?"

"One moment. I think she's just coming in."

"Hello." It was Monique's voice.

"I hope you're not too disappointed. It's not Albert, only the Chief Superintendent. There's just one thing I forgot to ask you. Which of you has the money?"

She was quick to grasp his meaning.

"I have."

"Where is it?"

"Here. I keep it locked in one of the drawers of my desk."

"Has he any money of his own?"

"Very little, I should think."

"Thanks. That's all I wanted to know."

Lucas was making signs to him indicating that he was wanted on another line. It was Janvier.

"Are you calling from Rue d'Angoulême?" asked Maigret in surprise.

"Not from the house. From the bistro on the corner."

"What's been happening?"

"I don't know if it was done on purpose, but I thought you ought to know. They've turned the room upside down and cleaned it thoroughly. The furniture and the floor are gleaming with polish, and there isn't a speck of dust anywhere."

"What about the top of the wardrobe?"

"That's been dusted, too. I could feel, from the way that woman looked at me, that she had put one over on me. I asked her when the cleaning had been done. She said that her charwoman was there yesterday afternoon—she only goes in twice a week—so she thought she'd take advantage of her being there to give the room a thorough housecleaning."

"You had said nothing about leaving it the way it was, she said, and as long as she'd have to rent it again . . ."

Maigret had made a blunder. He ought to have foreseen this.

"Where is Moers?"

"He's still up there, in the hope that one or two finger-prints at least may have been overlooked. He hasn't found anything yet. If it really was done by the charwoman, she's made a thorough job of it. Do you want me to come back to the Quai?"

"Not just yet. Find out the name and address of the char-woman, and go see her. Ask her to tell you exactly what happened, what her instructions were, whether anyone else was in the room with her . . ."

"I get it."

"Moers may as well give up. Just one more thing. Did you notice anyone from the vice squad watching the house?"

"Yes, Dumoncel. I've just spoken to him, as a matter of fact."

"Tell him to call Headquarters and ask for reinforcements. If any one of the women leaves the house, I want her followed."

"They're not ready to go out yet. One of them seems to have a mania for trailing up and down the stairs stark-naked, and another is having a bath. As for the third one, apparently no one has seen her for several days."

Maigret decided to go and see the Chief Commissioner, not for any particular reason, but just because, as sometimes happened, he felt like an informal chat about this case and other matters. He liked the atmosphere of the Chief's office. He always stood near the window to enjoy the view of Pont Saint-Michel and the Quais.

"Tired, are you?"

"I feel as if I've been playing an endless game of patience. I'm itching to be everywhere at once, so I end up just pacing up and down in my office. This morning I had one of the most . . ."

He paused, groping for the right word to describe his interview with Monique, but it eluded him. He felt bushed, or perhaps drained was a better word, as if he were suffering from a severe hang-over.

"And yet she was only a girl, scarcely more than a kid, really."

"The Thouret girl, do you mean?"

The telephone rang. The Chief Commissioner answered it. "Yes, he's here."

And, turning to Maigret:

"It's for you. Neveu has arrived, bringing someone with him. He can't wait to show you his prize."

"See you later, then."

As he went past the waiting room, he could see Inspector Neveu, on his feet, apparently in a state of great excitement, and sitting beside him, on one of the upright chairs, a pale, sickly-looking man of indeterminate age whose face seemed somehow familiar. It was more than that; he felt as if he had known the man all his life, yet he couldn't put a name to him.

"Do you want a word with me in private first?" he said to Neveu.

"There wouldn't be any point. And, besides, I wouldn't risk letting this character out of my sight for a single second."

It was only then that Maigret realized the man was hand-cuffed.

He went into his office, followed by the prisoner, who was dragging his feet a little. He smelled of liquor. Neveu, bringing up the rear, locked the door behind him and removed the handcuffs from the man's wrists.

"Don't you recognize him, Chief?"

Maigret still could not put a name to him. All the same, one thing was suddenly clear. The man had the look of a clown stripped of his make-up, cheeks that seemed to be made of rubber, a wide mouth twisted in an expression of bitterness mingled with drollery.

Who was it who had spoken recently of a man with a face like a clown? Mademoiselle Léone? The old bookkeeper, Monsieur Saimbron? At any rate, whoever it was, that person had seen Monsieur Louis sitting on a bench on Boulevard Saint-Martin or Boulevard Bonne-Nouvelle in the company of another man.

"Take a seat."

The man answered as if he felt completely at home.

"Thanks, Chief."

CHAPTER SEVEN

THE RAINWEAR SHOP

☐ "Jef Schrameck, otherwise known as Fred the Clown, also the Acrobat, born at Riquewihr, in the Upper Rhine, sixty-three years of age."

Flushed with triumph, Inspector Neveu introduced his captive with all the flourish of a ringmaster.

"Do you remember him now, Chief?"

Neveu was referring to something that had occurred fifteen years ago or more. Now that Maigret came to think of it, it had happened not so far from Boulevard·Saint-Martin, somewhere between Rue de Richelieu and·Rue Drouot.

"Sixty-three?" repeated Maigret, looking at the man, who, taking this as a compliment, responded with a broad smile.

Possibly, because he was so thin, he didn't look his age. In fact, he was ageless. It was his expression, most of all, that made it impossible to think of him as a man getting along in years. Terrified though he must be, he still looked as if he couldn't take anyone seriously, not even himself. No doubt it was simply a mannerism acquired over the years, like the capacity to make extraordinary faces. He just had to make people laugh.

The amazing thing was that he had been more than forty-five even back at the time of that business on the Boulevards, which had turned him into a celebrity for a few weeks.

Maigret pressed the buzzer and lifted the receiver of the interoffice telephone.

"Would you please send me down the file on Schrameck Jef Schrameck, born at Riquewihr, in the Upper Rhine."

He could not remember how it started. It had been an evening in early spring, for it was already pitch-dark by eight o'clock.

The Grands Boulevards had been crowded, and there was not a single vacant chair on any of the café terraces.

Had someone noticed a dim light flickering in one of the windows of an office building? At any rate, the police were alerted and came running to the spot. As usual, a crowd gathered, though most of the people had no idea what was going on.

No one dreamed that the spectacle would last nearly two hours and would provide so much drama interspersed with comic interludes, or that toward the end there would be such a crowd that it would become necessary to erect barricades.

Trapped in the office building, the intruder had opened a window and, with the help of a strip of gutter, had crawled sideways along the entire length of the façade. He had just found a foothold on the sill of a window on the floor above him when a policeman appeared. The man persisted with his hazardous climb, to the accompaniment of terrified shrieks from the women in the crowd below.

It was one of the most exciting chases in police history, with the pursuers inside the building hurrying from one floor to the next, flinging windows open as they went, and the quarry nimbly eluding them, as if performing a circus act entirely for his own amusement.

He was the first to reach the roof, a steeply sloping roof,

which the police had been reluctant to risk climbing. The man, apparently impervious to vertigo, took a flying leap onto the next roof, and so on from one building to the next, until he reached the corner of the Rue Drouot, where he vanished through a skylight.

They lost sight of him, but found him again, a quarter of an hour later, on another roof farther on. The people in the street pointed upward shouting: "There he is!"

No one knew what he had been doing in the first place or whether he was armed. Someone started a rumor that he had killed several people.

The climax of the show, as far as the spectators were concerned, was the arrival of the Fire Brigade with their ladders. Some time went by before powerful floodlights were set up and trained on the roof tops.

When at last he was arrested, in Rue de la Grange-Batelière, he was not even out of breath. He was very cocky and poured amiable scorn on the police. Then, at the very moment when he was being bundled into a car, he wriggled out of the grasp of his captors like an eel and managed, heaven knows how, to worm his way to freedom through the crowd.

The name of the man was Schrameck. For several days the Acrobat hogged the headlines in all the newspapers, until he was recaptured, quite by chance, at a race track.

He had made his debut as a circus performer at a very early age, appearing mainly in Germany and Alsace-Lorraine. Later he had come to Paris and, except for brief spells in prison for theft, had always been able to find employment at various fairgrounds.

"I never dreamed," Inspector Neveu was saying, "that he was spending his declining years in my territory."

The man remarked, in all seriousness:

"I turned over a new leaf years ago."

"I'd gotten a description of a tall, thin, elderly man who had been seen in conversation with Monsieur Louis on benches on the Boulevards."

Hadn't someone said to Maigret: "The sort of man you often see sitting on a bench"?

Fred the Clown was the kind of person you would not be the least bit surprised to find lounging around for hours watching the passers-by or feeding the pigeons. His coloring blended with the gray paving stones, and he had the look of a man who had nothing to do and nowhere to go.

"Before I hand him over to you, I think I ought to tell you how I happened to catch up with him. I was in a bar in Rue Blondel, very near Porte Saint-Martin. The bar also serves as a betting shop. It's called Chez Fernand. Fernand is a former jockey. I know him well. I showed him a photograph of Monsieur Louis, and I could tell from the way he looked at it that he recognized him."

" 'Is he a customer of yours?' I asked him.

" 'He isn't himself. But he's been in here two or three times with one of my best customers.'

" 'Who's that?'

" 'Fred the Clown.'

" 'The Acrobat? I thought he either had died long ago or was in prison!'

" 'He's very much alive, and he comes in here every afternoon for a glass of something and to place his bets. But, come to think of it, I haven't seen him for some days now.'

" 'How long, exactly?'

Fernand considered the matter, and then he went and had a word with his wife in the kitchen.

" 'Monday was the last time he came in.'

" 'Was Monsieur Louis with him?'

"He couldn't remember, but he was quite sure he hadn't set eyes on the Acrobat since last Monday. Do you see what I'm getting at?

"The next step was to find him. Now I knew where to look. I had found out the name of the woman he's been living with for the past few years. She used to sell vegetables off a barrow. Her name is Françoise Bidou.

"Then I only had to get her address. She lives on Quai de Valmy, overlooking the canal.

"I found my man lurking in her bedroom. He hadn't set foot outside since Monday. The first thing I did was to clap him in handcuffs. I didn't want him slipping through my fingers."

"I'm not as agile as I used to be," quipped Schrameck.

There was a knock on the door. A thick, buff-colored file was deposited on Maigret's desk. It contained Schrameck's life history, or, more precisely, the history of his brushes with the law.

Unhurriedly, puffing at his pipe, Maigret leafed through it.

As far as he was concerned, this was the best time of day for conducting interviews. Between twelve and two most of the offices were deserted, and there were fewer interruptions and hardly any telephone calls. He had the same feeling he had often experienced late at night, of having the whole place to himself.

"You must be hungry," he said to Neveu.

Since Neveu seemed at a loss as to how to reply, Maigret persisted.

"You'd better go out and have a snack now. I may want you to relieve me here later."

"Whatever you say, Chief."

Neveu, much against his will, went out. The prisoner

watched him go with a mocking expression on his face. Maigret lighted a fresh pipe, laid his broad hand on the file, looked Fred the Clown straight in the eye, and murmured:

"Alone, at last!"

He felt more at his ease with this man than he had with Monique. All the same, before getting down to business he took the precaution of locking his door, and even went so far as to bolt the door connecting with the inspectors' duty room. Then, catching Maigret glancing at the window, Jef protested, with a comic grimace:

"Don't be afraid. I'm past keeping my balance on narrow ledges."

"I suppose you know why you're here?"

Ever the clown, he protested plaintively:

"It's always the same people who get arrested! It reminds me of the good old days. Nothing like this has happened to me for years."

"Your friend Louis has been murdered. It's no good putting on that bewildered expression. You know very well who I mean. You are also well aware that there's every likelihood of your being charged with having committed the crime."

"That would be just one more miscarriage of justice."

Maigret picked up the telephone.

"Get me Chez Fernand. It's a bar in Rue Blondel."

When he had Fernand on the line, he said:

"Chief Superintendent Maigret speaking. It's about one of your regulars, Jef Schrameck . . . The Acrobat, that's right . . . I want to know whether he gambled heavily . . . What? . . . Yes, I see . . . And lately? . . . Saturday? . . . I'm much obliged to you . . . No . . . That's all for the present."

He seemed satisfied. Jef, on the other hand, was looking a little uneasy.

"Do you want me to repeat what I have just been told?"

"People will say anything!"

"All your life you've been losing money on the horses."

"If the government had put a stop to it, I would have been spared the expense."

"You've been betting with Fernand for some years now."

"He's a registered bookie."

"Be that as it may, you must have got the money to bet with from somewhere. Now, until about two and a half years ago you bet only in very small sums. On occasion you didn't even have enough to pay for your drinks, and Fernand would let you have them on credit."

"He shouldn't have done it! It only encouraged me to keep at it."

"Then, all of a sudden, you began staking larger sums of money, sometimes very large sums. And a few days later you would be cleaned out all over again."

"What does that prove?"

"Last Saturday you staked an enormous sum."

"What of it? The owners are often ready to risk as much as a million francs on a horse!"

"Where did you get the money?"

"My wife is working."

"What does she do?"

"Housework. Occasionally she helps out in one of the bistros on the Quai."

"Do you take me for a fool?"

"Such a thought never crossed my mind, Chief Superintendent."

"Now, look here, we've wasted enough time already."

"I assure you, I have no pressing engagements . . ."

"Never mind that. I'm going to tell you just where you stand. You were seen by several witnesses in Monsieur Louis's company."

"A finer man you couldn't wish to meet."

"That's neither here nor there. I don't mean recently. This was about two and a half years ago. At that time, Monsieur Louis had been out of work for months. He was at the end of his rope."

"I know the feeling all too well," sighed Jef. "However long the rope, we all come to the end of it sometime!"

"As for what you were living on in those days, I have no idea, but I'm prepared to believe that you were being kept by your friend Françoise. You hung around on benches, occasionally venturing a few francs on a horse and getting your drinks on credit in various bars. As for Monsieur Louis, he was driven to borrowing money from at least two old friends."

"Which only goes to show that the world is full of people down on their luck."

Maigret ignored this remark. Jef had been accustomed to the laughter of an audience for so long that he had developed a craving for it, which was why he could never stop clowning. Doggedly, the Chief Superintendent pursued his own line of reasoning.

"The fact remains that all of a sudden you were both very flush. The evidence, with exact dates, will emerge in the course of the inquiry."

"I can never remember dates."

"After that, there were times when you gambled heavily, and others when you couldn't even pay for your drinks. Nobody could fail to draw the conclusion that you and Monsieur Louis had found a means of laying your hands on very large sums of money. Whatever the means, it was not legal. But we'll come to that later."

"What a pity! I'm dying to hear how we managed it."

"You'll soon be laughing on the other side of your face. I repeat that on Saturday you were loaded with money, but you lost it all in the space of a few hours. On Monday afternoon, your associate, Monsieur Louis, was murdered in an alley off Boulevard Saint-Martin."

"It was a tragic loss for me."

"Have you ever been up for trial at the assizes?"

"No. Only in the lower courts. Several times."

"Well, I may as well tell you that juries as a rule don't care much for clowning, especially from a man with your record. Nothing is more calculated to persuade them that you were the only person who knew where to find Monsieur Louis at all times of day, and the only one with a motive for his murder."

"In that case, they must be a lot of idiots."

"That's all I have to say to you. It is now half past twelve. We are both here in my office. At one o'clock Examining Magistrate Coméliau will be back in his chambers.

"As soon as he arrives, I'll hand you over to him, and he will deal with you as he thinks fit."

"Isn't he a little dark man with a toothbrush moustache?"

"Yes."

"He and I have met before. He's a real so-and-so. Come to think of it, he can't be so young any more. What if I say I don't want to see him?"

"It rests entirely with you, as you very well know."

Jef the Clown heaved a long sigh.

"You don't by any chance happen to have a spare cigarette?"

Maigret took a pack from his drawer and held it out to him.

"Have you a match?"

Jef smoked for a while in silence.

"I don't suppose you keep any liquor in here?"

"Are you going to come clean?"

"I'm not sure yet. I'm still considering whether there's anything I can usefully say."

This might turn out to be a very long session. Maigret knew his kind. On an impulse, he went across to the door leading to the inspectors' room and called out:

"Lucas! Do me a favor. Go to Quai de Valny and find a woman called Françoise Bidou. I want her brought here."

At this the Clown wriggled in his chair and held up his hand like a schoolboy in the classroom.

"You wouldn't do that to me, Chief Superintendent!"

"Will you talk?"

"It would help a lot if I could have a little something to drink."

"Hold on, Lucas. Don't go until I tell you."

And to Jef:

"Are you afraid of your wife?"

"You promised to give me a drink."

Maigret shut the door, went to the cupboard, and got out the bottle of brandy that he always kept there. He poured a small shot into a tumbler.

"Aren't you going to join me?"

"Well, what have you got to say?"

"Ask me whatever questions you like. I'd appreciate it if you would take note that I am making no attempt to impede the course of justice, as the lawyers put it."

"Where did you first meet Monsieur Louis?"

"On a bench in Boulevard Bonne-Nouvelle."

"How did you strike up an acquaintance with him?"

"The way anyone does sitting next to someone on a bench. I remarked on the weather, and he agreed that it was cold for early spring, but said that it was milder than it had been the week before."

"Would this have been about two and a half years ago?"

"Something like that. I didn't make a note of the date in my diary. We met every day on the same bench after that. He seemed glad to have someone to talk to."

"Did he mention that he was out of work?"

"By degrees, he told me the whole story of his life. He said he'd been with the same firm twenty-five years and that the boss had then decided, without a word of warning to anyone, to close down the business. He said he hadn't dared tell his wife—just between ourselves, she sounds like a real cow—and she believed he was still working at the same job. I imagine it was the first chance he'd had to get it all off his chest, and it was a great relief to him."

"Did he know who you were?"

"All I told him was that I used to be a circus performer."

"And then?"

"What exactly do you want to know?"

"Everything."

"I'd be obliged if you'd take another look at my file first and tot up the number of convictions. What I want to know is whether this new charge is likely to get me transported. I wouldn't like that."

Maigret did as he was asked.

"Unless the charge is murder, you're still two short of the requisite number of convictions."

"That's what I thought. I wasn't sure your total would tally with mine."

"What was the racket? Stealing?"

"It wasn't as simple as that."

"Whose idea was it?"

"His, of course. I haven't got the wits to dream up a scheme like that. Don't you think I've earned another little drop?"

"When I've heard all you have to tell me."

"That's going to take a long time. Well, you leave me with no choice but to cut it as short as possible."

The Chief Superintendent yielded and poured him another mouthful of brandy.

"As a matter of fact, it was the bench that first gave him the idea."

"How do you mean?"

"Since he spent most of his time sitting on a bench, usually the same bench, he began to take notice of his surroundings. Do you, by any chance, know the shop on the boulevard where they sell raincoats?"

"I know the one you mean."

"The bench where Louis usually sat was just across from it. So, almost without realizing it, he became very familiar with the comings and goings in the shop and with the habits of the employees. And that's what put the idea into his head. When you have the whole day ahead of you, and nothing to do, you get to thinking. You plan projects, even projects that haven't a prayer of being realized. One day he began telling me about one of these projects of his, just to pass the time. That particular shop is always crowded. It sells nothing but raincoats, of every shape and size, raincoats for men, women, and children. The children's coats are tucked away in a corner. And there are more upstairs. On the left of the building, as with so many in that district, there is a little alleyway leading to a courtyard.

"Would you like me to draw you a diagram?" he suggested.

"Not now. Go on."

"Louis said to me:

"*'I'm surprised no one has ever robbed the till. It would be the easiest thing in the world.'*"

"You couldn't wait to hear more, I daresay."

"Naturally, I was interested. He explained to me that at

about twelve, or a quarter past at the latest, everyone was shooed out of the shop and the employees all went off to lunch. And that included the boss, a little old man with a wisp of a beard, who always lunched at the Chope du Nègre, not far from where we were sitting.

" 'Suppose one of the customers was to stay behind and get locked in?'

"Don't you say it couldn't be done. My first reaction, too, was that it was impossible. But Louis had been studying the layout of the shop for weeks. The staff never bothered to look in all the dark corners or behind the racks of raincoats to satisfy themselves that there was no one left in the shop. It never occurred to them that anyone might stay behind on purpose, see?

"Everything depended on that. The boss was always the last to leave, locking the door carefully behind him."

"And you were the one to stay behind, I suppose? And after that, all you had to do was force the lock and slip away with the takings?"

"You're quite mistaken. And that's what made it such a lark. Even if I'd got caught, they wouldn't have found a shred of evidence. Admittedly, I did empty the till. After that I went into the lavatories. Next to the urinals there is a tiny skylight, too small even for a child of three to squeeze through, but quite big enough for throwing out a parcel of money. It overlooks the courtyard. As if by sheer chance, Louis was passing by underneath and he picked up the parcel. As for me, all I had to do was wait until the staff returned and there were enough customers in the shop for me to slip out unnoticed the same way I came in. Which is what I did."

"How did you divide up the money?"

"Fifty-fifty, like brothers. The hardest thing was to persuade Louis to make up his mind. The whole plan was just an

imaginary exercise to him. He took pride in it, the way a painter
does in his work. When I first suggested that we should put
it into practice, he was shocked. What finally tipped the scales
was the thought of having to tell his wife that he was flat
broke. You will have noticed that the plan had one further
advantage. It's true that, having admitted the offense, I will be
convicted of theft, but, since there was no breaking and enter-
ing, that will mean, if I'm not mistaken, two years lopped off
my sentence."

"I'll have a look at the Criminal Code later."

"Well, I've told you all there is to tell. Louis and I did
very nicely out of it, and I have no regrets. The proceeds of
that little venture kept us going for over three months. Well,
to be perfectly frank, my share didn't last quite that long, on
account of all those broken-down nags, but Louis used to slip
me a bill from time to time.

"When we realized we were coming to the end of our
resources, we moved to a different bench."

"With the intention of planning another job?"

"Well, why not? The scheme was an excellent one, and
there was no point in trying anything new. Now that you know
the trick, you only have to look through the files to spot all the
jobs I pulled off by getting myself locked into a shop. The next
time it was a shop that sold electrical goods, on the same boulevard but a bit higher up. There was no alley, but the back of
the shop overlooked the courtyard of the building opposite,
which was just as good. In that district, the lavatories nearly
always have a small window or vent overlooking a courtyard or
passageway.

"I was only caught once, by a salesgirl who opened a
closet I was hiding in. I pretended to be falling-down drunk.
She called the manager, and the two of them hustled me out,
threatening to call the police if I didn't clear out.

"Now, will you be so good as to explain what possible motive I could have had for killing Louis? We were buddies. I even introduced him to Françoise, to reassure her, because she was beginning to wonder what I was up to. He brought her a box of chocolates, and she thought he was most distinguished."

"Did you pull off a job last week?"

"It was in all the papers. A dress shop on Boulevard Montmartre."

"I take it that when Louis was killed he was in the alley to check that there was a suitable window at the back of the jeweler's overlooking the courtyard?"

"Very likely. He was always the one to case the joint, because of his respectable appearance. People tend to be more suspicious of a man like me. Even when I'm dressed to the nines, they look sideways at me."

"Who killed him?"

"Why ask me?"

"Who would have had a motive for killing him?"

"I don't know. His wife, maybe."

"Why should his wife have wanted to kill him?"

"I told you she was a real cow. Supposing she'd found out that he'd been thumbing his nose at her for over two years and that he had a lady friend . . ."

"Do you know her?"

"He never introduced me to her, but he often talked about her, and I saw her once or twice from a distance. He was very fond of her. He was a man who needed affection. Well, come to think of it, don't we all? I've got my Françoise. I daresay you've got someone of your own, too. They got along very well. They used to go to the movies, or else they'd go to a café and chat."

"Did she know what was going on?"

"I'm sure she didn't."

"Who did know?"

"I did, for a start."

"That's obvious."

"His daughter, possibly. He worried a lot about his daughter. He said that the older she got, the more like her mother she was. She was always badgering him for money."

"Did you ever go to see him in Rue d'Angoulême?"

"Never."

"But you knew the house?"

"He pointed it out to me."

"Why didn't you ever go in?"

"Because I didn't want to spoil things for him. His landlady thought he was a very respectable man. If she'd seen me . . ."

"What if I were to tell you that we've found your fingerprints in his room?"

"I would reply that fingerprints are a load of tripe."

He talked as if he hadn't a care in the world. He believed he was on a winning streak. Every now and then he would take a quick look at the bottle.

"Who else knew?"

"See here, Chief Superintendent, I am what I am, but I've never squealed in all my life."

"You mean you'd rather take the rap yourself?"

"That would be a miscarriage of justice."

"Who else knew?"

"The young madam's boyfriend. Now, there's one for you. I wouldn't stake a fortune on his innocence. I don't know whether he was acting on orders from his ladylove, but he took to following Louis in the afternoon for days at a time. He went to see him twice, to extort money from him. Louis was scared stiff the kid would blab to his wife or write her an anonymous letter."

"Do you know him?"

"No. I know he's very young and that he works in a book-shop in the mornings. Lately, Louis was haunted by a sense of impending catastrophe. He said that things couldn't go on as they were and that his wife was bound to learn the truth in the end."

"Did he ever mention his brothers-in-law?"

"Often. They were always being held up to him as an ex-ample. They were made use of to show him up as a failure, a good-for-nothing, a namby-pamby, a nobody. He was told that if he was so content with his miserable lot, he ought never to have married. It was a shock to me, I can tell you."

"What was?"

"Reading in the paper that he was dead. Especially be-cause I wasn't very far away when it happened. Fernand will confirm that I was in his bar having a drink at the time."

"Did Louis carry much money on him?"

"I don't know about that, but I do know that two days earlier we had pulled off quite a lucrative job."

"Was he in the habit of carrying the money around with him?"

"Either that or he'd leave it in his room. The joke was that every evening he had to go back to his room to change his shoes and tie before catching his train. One time he forgot his tie. He told me all this himself. It was only when he got to the Gare de Lyon that he noticed it. He couldn't go out and buy just any other tie. It had to be the same one he'd been wearing when he left home in the morning. He had to go all the way back to Rue d'Angoulême, and when he got home he made up a story about having been kept late at work to see to some rush job or other."

"Why have you been hiding in Françoise's room since Tuesday?"

"What would you have done in my place? When I read

the paper on Tuesday morning, I realized that someone would have seen Louis and me together sometime and that they'd be sure to tell the police. They always pick on people of my sort, anyway."

"Did you never consider leaving Paris?"

"No, I just lay low, in the hope that they wouldn't get on to me. This morning, when I heard your inspector calling out to me, I knew I was done for."

"Does Françoise know what you've been up to?"

"No."

"How does she suppose you managed to get hold of all that money?"

"To begin with, she hasn't seen much of it, only what I had left after my racing losses. And then she believes I'm still picking pockets in the Métro."

"Is that what you used to do?"

"Surely you don't expect me to answer that. By the way, don't you ever get thirsty?"

Maigret poured him another shot.

"Are you quite sure there's nothing you haven't told me?"

"As sure as I'm sitting here!"

Maigret opened the door to the inspectors' room and called out to Lucas:

"Take him down to the cells."

Then, looking toward Jef Schrameck, who stood up with a sigh, he added:

"He'd better be handcuffed, just to be on the safe side."

As he was going out, the Acrobat turned around with an odd little smile on his mobile face, and Maigret said:

"Tell them not to be too hard on him."

"Thank you, Chief Superintendent. Oh! There's one other thing. Please don't tell Françoise that I gambled away all that money. She's quite capable of punishing me by not sending me any little extras in prison."

Maigret put on his coat, took his hat down from the hook, and decided to go to the Brasserie Dauphine for a bite to eat. He was going down the main staircase, which was, as usual, gray with dust, when he heard the sounds of a scuffle coming from the ground floor. He looked over the banister.

A young man, with his hair flying all over the place, was struggling in the grip of a giant of a constable with a bleeding scratch on his cheek. The constable was growling:

"Cool it, kiddo, if you don't want a smack in the chops!"

The Chief Superintendent was sorely tempted to laugh. It was Albert Jorisse, on his unwilling way to see him. He was still struggling and shouting:

"Let go of me! I told you, I won't run away . . ."

At this point, the two of them came face to face with Maigret on the stairs.

"I arrested him a couple of minutes ago on Pont Saint-Michel. I knew him at once. When I apprehended him, he tried to get away."

"That's not true! He's lying!"

The young man was red in the face and panting, and his eyes were feverishly bright. The policeman had a grip on his coat collar, which he had pulled up high, as if he were manipulating a puppet.

"Tell him to let go of me."

He kicked out with his foot, but missed.

"I told you I wanted to see Chief Superintendent Maigret. I came here, didn't I? I came here of my own free will."

His clothes were crumpled, his trousers still streaked with mud after yesterday's downpour. He had huge black circles under his eyes.

"I am Chief Superintendent Maigret."

"Well, then, order him to let go of me."

"It's all right, son, you can let go now."

"Whatever you say, sir, but . . ."

The constable was convinced that the young man was as slippery as an eel.

"He's a big bully," panted Albert Jorisse. "He treated me as if . . . as if . . ."

He was stammering with rage.

Smiling in spite of himself, the Chief Superintendent pointed to the constable's bleeding cheek.

"It looks to me rather as if he was the one who . . ."

Jorisse, who had not noticed the gash until now, looked at the constable with flashing eyes and shouted:

"Serves him right!"

CHAPTER EIGHT

MONIQUE'S
SECRET

☐ "Sit down, you young ruffian."

"I'm not a young ruffian," protested Jorisse.

He had still not quite got his breath back and was wheezing a little, but he had calmed down a lot.

"I wouldn't have expected it of you, Chief Superintendent Maigret, using insulting language like that before even giving me time to explain."

Maigret, somewhat taken aback, looked at him, frowning.

"Have you had any lunch?"

"I'm not hungry."

He spoke like a sulky kid.

"Hello," Maigret said into the phone. "Get me the Brasserie Dauphine . . . Hello. Is that you, Joseph? . . . Maigret here . . . I'd be obliged if you'd bring over some sandwiches. Six . . . Ham for me . . . Just a minute . . ."

And to Jorisse:

"Ham or cheese?"

"I don't really mind. Ham."

"Beer or red wine?"

"I'd be glad for some water. I'm thirsty."

"Joseph? Six ham sandwiches, cut nice and thick, and four beers . . . Hang on a second . . . You may as well bring us two cups of black coffee while you're at it . . . And be as quick as you can, won't you?"

He replaced the receiver, and then immediately lifted it again and dialed an inside number, never taking his eyes off the young man, whose appearance interested him. Jorisse was thin and frail-looking, jumpy to the point of neurosis, suggesting that his staple diet was black coffee rather than nourishing steaks. Otherwise he wasn't bad-looking, with his long brown hair, which he had to shake out of his eyes by tossing his head every now and then.

Perhaps because he was still very worked up, his nostrils twitched occasionally. He was still looking reproachfully at the Chief Superintendent, with his head to one side.

"Hello. You can call off the search for Jorisse. Pass the message on to all the police and railroad stations."

The youth opened his mouth, but Maigret didn't give him time to speak.

"Later!"

The sky was once more overcast. There was more rain in the offing. No doubt it would come down in buckets, as it had on the day of the funeral. Maigret went over to the window and shut it, and then, still without a word, he returned to his desk and rearranged his pipes, as a typist, before getting down to work, rearranges her machine, her shorthand pad, and her carbons.

There was a knock on the door.

"Come in," he said testily.

It was Inspector Neveu. . . . He just put his head in the door, assuming that the Chief was in the middle of an interrogation.

"Excuse me. I just wanted to ask what . . ."

"You can leave now. Oh, and thanks!"

When he had gone, the Chief Superintendent began pacing up and down, to fill in the time until the waiter arrived from the Brasserie Dauphine. He also made another telephone call, this time to his wife:

"I won't be in for lunch."

"I was beginning to wonder. Do you know what time it is?"

"No. Does it matter?"

She burst out laughing. He couldn't imagine why.

"I came here to tell you . . ."

"It'll keep."

It was his third interrogation that day. He was thirsty. Then he noticed, all of a sudden, that the young man was staring at the bottle of brandy and the used tumbler that had been left standing on his desk.

Maigret blushed like a child and only just stopped himself from blurting out that it wasn't he who had been drinking brandy out of a tall glass, but Jef Schrameck, who had left the office moments before Albert arrived.

Had the boy's reproachful words struck home? Was Chief Superintendent Maigret regretting that he had tarnished the boy's image of him?

"Come in, Joseph. Put the tray down on the desk. Everything's there, I take it?"

And when at last they were alone with the tray of food:

"Let's eat."

Jorisse ate heartily, in spite of having said that he wasn't hungry. All through the meal he kept darting inquiring glances at the Chief Superintendent, but by the time he had finished his first glass of beer, he seemed to have regained a little self-confidence.

"Feeling better?"

"Yes, thanks. All the same, you did call me a ruffian."

"We'll discuss that later."

"It really is true that I was on my way to see you."

"What for?"

"Because I was sick of running away."

"Why did you run away?"

"So as not to get myself arrested."

"Why should anyone have wanted to arrest you?"

"You know very well why."

"No, I don't."

"Because I am Monique's friend."

"Why were you so sure we'd find out?"

"You were bound to."

"And you think that because you and Monique are friends, we would have arrested you?"

"You wanted to make me talk."

"I did, to be sure!"

"You've made up your mind that I'm going to lie to you, and you won't be happy until you've tripped me up."

"I'm afraid you've been reading too many detective stories."

"No. But I read the papers. I know how you people go about things."

"In that case, what exactly are you doing here?"

"I've come to tell you that I didn't kill Monsieur Louis Thouret."

Maigret, puffing at his pipe, slowly sipped his second glass of beer. He was seated at his desk. The green-shaded light was switched on, and the first few drops of rain were spreading on the windowpanes.

"Do you understand the implications of what you have just said?"

"I don't know what you mean."

"You assumed that you were under threat of arrest. Which

means that there were good reasons why we should arrest you."

"You've been to Rue d'Angoulême, haven't you?"

"How do you know that?"

"You found out by the merest chance that he had a room in town. It was because of the brown shoes, wasn't it?"

The Chief Superintendent looked at him with an amused little smile.

"So what?"

"The woman there must surely have told you that I'd been to see him."

"Is that any reason why we should have arrested you?"

"You've interrogated Monique."

"Do you really believe she would give you away?"

"It wouldn't surprise me to learn that you'd managed to make her talk."

"In that case, what was the point of hiding under a friend's bed?"

"So you know that, too?"

"Please answer my question."

"I wasn't thinking. I panicked. I was afraid I might be browbeaten into saying things that weren't true."

"Did you get that from the newspapers, as well?"

After all, hadn't René Lecoeur's lawyer referred in open court to the brutality of the police, and hadn't the words been quoted in every newspaper in the land? In fact, there had been a letter from Lecoeur that morning. In despair at being under sentence of death, he had written to beg the Chief Superintendent to visit him in prison.

Maigret was tempted to show the letter to the youngster. He would do so later if it proved necessary.

"Why didn't you remain in hiding in Rue Gay-Lussac?"

"Because I couldn't stand to spend the whole day hiding

under a bed. It was ghastly. I ached all over. I kept thinking all the time that I was going to sneeze. It's a small apartment and all the doors are left open. I could hear my friend's aunt moving around the whole time. If I'd so much as moved, she would have been sure to hear me."

"Is that the only reason?"

"I was hungry."

"What did you do?"

"I wandered around the streets. At night, I managed to get a couple of hours' sleep by lying on a sack of vegetables in Les Halles. Twice I got as far as Pont Saint-Michel. I saw Monique come out of this building. I walked to Rue d'Angoulême, and there was a man there who looked as if he were watching the house. I assumed he must be from the police."

"What reason would you have had for killing Monsieur Louis?"

"Don't you know that I borrowed money from him?"

"Borrowed?"

"All right, I asked him for money, if you like."

"Asked?"

"What are you suggesting?"

"There are different ways of asking. Among others, there is a way that makes it almost impossible for the person concerned to refuse. In plain terms, blackmail."

He was silent, gazing fixedly at the floor.

"What do you have to say to that?"

"In actual fact, I would never have told Madame Thouret."

"All the same, you threatened to?"

"That wasn't necessary."

"Because a hint that you might talk was enough?"

"I don't know. You're confusing me."

He added, in a weary voice:

"I'm dead on my feet."

"Drink your coffee."

He obeyed meekly, never taking his eyes off Maigret.

"How often did you go to see him?"

"Only twice."

"Did Monique know?"

"What did she say about it?"

"Never you mind what she said. I want to get at the truth."

"She did know."

"What did you say to him?"

"To whom?"

"To Louis Thouret, of course."

"That we needed money."

"Who's 'we'?"

"Monique and I."

"What did you say you wanted it for?"

"To go to South America."

"So you told him you intended to run away together?"

"Yes."

"How did he react?"

"In the end he agreed that he had no choice in the matter."

There was something wrong somewhere. It was beginning to dawn on Maigret that the youngster thought he knew more than he actually did. He would have to be careful.

"Did you ask his permission to marry her?"

"Yes. But he knew very well it was out of the question. First, I am under age and would have to get my parents' consent. Second, even if they were to agree, Madame Thouret would never have put up with a son-in-law who still had to make a career for himself. Monsieur Thouret himself was the first to discourage me from approaching his wife."

"Did you tell him that you and Monique had been making love in heaven knows how many different hotel rooms?"

"I didn't go into details."

For the second time he blushed.

"I simply told him that she was pregnant."

Maigret didn't start or give any other sign of surprise. All the same, it was a shock. He blamed his own lack of insight. Because it was, he had to admit, the one possibility that had never occurred to him.

"How far along is she?"

"Just over two months."

"You've seen a doctor, I presume?"

"She wouldn't let me go in with her."

"But she has seen someone?"

"Yes."

"Did you wait for her outside?"

"No."

Maigret changed his position slightly and began mechanically to fill another pipe.

"What did you have in mind to do when you got to South America?"

"Anything at all. I'm not afraid of work. I could have become a cowboy."

He said this with great seriousness, even a touch of pride, and Maigret had a mental image of the many six-foot roughnecks he had encountered on ranches in Texas and Arizona.

"A cowboy," he echoed.

"Or I could have prospected for gold."

"Of course!"

"I would have managed somehow."

"And you and Monique would have gotten married?"

"Yes. I imagine it would be easier there than here."

"Do you love Monique?"

"She's my wife, or as good as, isn't she? Just because we haven't been through the formalities . . ."

"How did Monsieur Louis react to this news?"

"He couldn't believe his daughter would do such a thing. He cried."

"In your presence?"

"Yes. I swore to him that my intentions . . ."

"Were honorable. Of course. What happened then?"

"He promised he'd help us. He couldn't give us all the money right away, but he gave me some."

"Where is this money?"

"Monique has it. She keeps it hidden in the desk in her office."

"What about the rest of the money?"

"He promised he'd let me have it on Tuesday. He was expecting a large payment."

"Who from?"

"I don't know."

"Didn't he tell you how he earned his money?"

"He couldn't, obviously."

"Why not?"

"Because he didn't have a job. I was never able to find out how he got the money. There were two of them involved."

"Did you ever see the other one?"

"Once, on the boulevard."

"A tall, thin man, with a face of a clown?"

"Yes."

"He was with me here until just a few minutes before you arrived. The brandy was for him."

"In that case, you know it all."

"What I want to know is whether you do."

"I don't know anything. My guess is that they were black-mailing someone."

"And you didn't see any reason why you shouldn't have a share of the loot?"

"We needed money, on account of the baby."

Maigret lifted the receiver of the interoffice telephone.

"Lucas? I want you in here for a moment."

As soon as Lucas arrived, Maigret introduced the young man.

"This is Albert Jorisse. He and Monique are expecting a baby."

He spoke with great solemnity, and Lucas, who did not know what to think, nodded.

"The young lady may still be in her office, since she wasn't able to be there this morning. I want you to go and get her, and then take her to a doctor. Let her decide which one. If she has no preference, it might as well be the one at the Préfecture. I want to know how many months pregnant she is."

"What if she refuses to be examined?"

"Tell her that if she does refuse I will have no choice but to arrest her, as well as her boyfriend, who is here in my office. Take a car. And telephone and let me know what she says."

When they were alone again, Jorisse asked:

"What was that all about?"

"It's my job to check up on everything."

"Don't you believe me?"

"I believe *you*, yes."

"But you don't believe her, is that it?"

The ringing of the telephone saved Maigret the embarrassment of replying. The call had nothing to do with the matter at hand. It concerned a lunatic who had been in to see him some days earlier and who had later been arrested in the street for riotous behavior. Instead of answering the caller in a few words, as he could have done, Maigret spun out the conversation for as long as possible.

When he had replaced the receiver, he asked, pretending that he had forgotten where they were:

"What do you intend to do now?"

"Do you accept my assurance that I didn't kill him?"

"I've always known that. You see, it's not as easy as is generally supposed to stab someone in the back. It's even more difficult to prevent the victim from crying out."

"You mean I would be incapable of doing it?"

"Sure."

He seemed almost offended. After all, he had had dreams of becoming a cowboy or a gold prospector in South America.

"Do you intend to go and see Madame Thouret?"

"I suppose I'll have to."

Maigret was sorely tempted to burst out laughing at the thought of the lad going to the house in Juvisy, his tail between his legs, in an attempt to butter up Monique's mother.

"Do you believe that, as things stand, she'll be prepared to regard you as an acceptable son-in-law?"

"I don't know."

"You don't deny, do you, that you didn't play it altogether straight?"

"What do you mean?"

"It isn't only that you asked Monsieur Louis to give you the money to take Monique to South America, but that, knowing Monique spends every afternoon going from house to house collecting debts, you decided you might as well take advantage of that fact.

"She could always hurry through her rounds with an hour or two to spare, which she got into the habit of spending shut up with you in some hotel room or other."

"We did meet like that sometimes."

"In order to do so, you were forced to give up your afternoon shift in the bookshop. And hotel rooms cost money."

"We did spend a little of . . ."

"You knew where Monsieur Louis kept his money, didn't you?"

He was watching the young man closely. He answered, without a moment's hesitation:

"On top of his glass-fronted wardrobe."

"When he gave you the money, did he get it from there?"

"Yes. But Monique had already told me about it."

"I take it you never went near the house in Rue d'Angoulême on Monday?"

"No, I didn't. Ask the landlady, if you like. I had an appointment to go and see him on Tuesday at five."

"When were you intending to leave for South America?"

"There's a ship sailing in three weeks. That would have given us time to get our visas. I've already applied for a passport."

"I thought that in the case of a minor parental consent was obligatory."

"I forged my father's signature."

There was a pause. Then, for the first time, Jorisse asked permission to smoke.

Maigret nodded. The absurd thing was that, having had his coffee, he really was longing now for a brandy, but he didn't have the courage to take out the bottle, which was back in the cupboard.

"You called me a ruffian."

"Don't you think you deserved it?"

"I had no choice but to do what I did."

"How would you like it if your son were to behave the way you did?"

"I intend to bring up my son differently. He won't have to . . ."

Once again they were interrupted by the telephone.

"Is that you, Chief?"

Maigret frowned. It was Neveu. He had not sent him out on any assignment.

"I've got the money!"

"You must be joking!"

He glanced at Jorisse, and said to the Inspector:

"Just a second. I'll get on the other line."

He went into the adjoining room and told the first inspector he saw to go in and keep an eye on the young man.

"That's better. Now you can talk freely. Where are you?"

"In a bistro on Quai de Valmy."

"What are you doing there?"

"You're not angry with me?"

"Go on."

"I meant it for the best. It's ten years now since Jef moved in with Françoise. From all I hear, he's fonder of her than he likes to admit. I suddenly had the urge to take a look around her place."

"What for?"

"I thought it was odd that he would have left her without any money. I was lucky enough to find her at home. There are only two rooms, plus a kind of closet they use as a kitchen. In the bedroom there is an iron bedstand with brass knobs. The walls are whitewashed, country style, but it's all very clean."

Feeling a little cross, Maigret waited for Neveu to finish his story. He didn't care for overzealousness, especially on the part of someone like Neveu, who belonged to a different branch of the service.

"Did you tell her Jef had been arrested?"

"Shouldn't I have?"

"Go on."

"To begin with, judging by her reactions, I was convinced she didn't know what he'd been up to. Her first thought was that I must have caught him picking pockets in the Métro or on a bus. Presumably that's his usual racket."

It was one of the many talents cultivated by Schrameck when he was still working around fairgrounds. One of his convictions had been for purse-stealing.

"Ignoring her protests, I set about searching the place. It wasn't until right at the end that it occurred to me to unscrew the brass knobs on the bed. They're hollow inside, and two of them were stuffed full of tightly rolled bills. They add up to a fortune! Françoise couldn't believe her eyes.

" *'To think that he let me go out doing housework when he had all that money hidden away! He'll never get to heaven! Just let him come back here, and he'll see what . . .'*

"She's still in the most fearful rage, calling him every name under the sun. She didn't even calm down when I suggested that he might have put the money aside to provide for her, in case anything happened to him.

" *'What amazes me,'* she snarled, *'is how he managed to avoid gambling it all away.'*

"Do you see what I'm getting at now, Chief? They must have had a big sharing-out last Saturday. I've got more than two hundred thousand francs here. Jef wouldn't have dared to gamble that much away, especially at Fernand's place. He only lost a fraction of the money. If they split it down the middle, Monsieur Louis must have had a bundle salted away, as well."

"I'm very grateful to you."

"What shall I do with the money?"

"Have you got it with you?"

"I should say I have! I couldn't very well leave it there . . ."

"Go and have a word with your Chief Superintendent, and ask him to get things sorted out according to the rule book."

"Must I?"

"Good heavens! I don't want the defense lawyers accusing us of having planted the notes!"

"Have I put my foot in it?"

"You have, rather."

"I'm sorry. I only wanted . . ."

Maigret hung up. He turned to Torrence, who was working at his desk.

"Are you very busy?"

"It's nothing that can't wait."

"I want you to go and see Chief Superintendent Antoine. Ask him to arrange for one of his men to make up a list of all the thefts committed in shops on the Grands Boulevards during the last two and a half years or so, especially those that took place when the shops were closed for lunch."

Such cases were not the concern of his department, but of Antoine's, whose office was at the end of the corridor.

He went back to Albert Jorisse, who had just lighted another cigarette, and released the inspector who had been keeping an eye on him.

"I had no intention of running away, you know."

"I daresay. But you might have been tempted to take a peek at the files on my desk. Go on, you may as well admit it."

"Perhaps."

"That makes all the difference."

"What does?"

"Never mind. I know what I'm talking about."

"What do you intend to do with me?"

"For the time being, you're staying here with me."

Maigret glanced at his watch and calculated that Lucas and Monique must have arrived at the doctor's by now. No doubt they were in the waiting room reading the magazines.

"You despise me, don't you?"

Maigret shrugged.

"I've never had a chance."

"A chance to do what?"

"To escape."

"To escape from what?"

Maigret sounded almost aggressive.

"You don't understand, I can see that. If you'd heard nothing but money, money, money, ever since you were a child, and if you'd seen your mother shaking with anxiety at the end of every month . . ."

"I had·no mother."

The boy was silenced. For nearly six minutes, not a word was spoken. For a while Maigret stood by the window, with his back to the room, watching the rain trickling down the windowpanes. Then he began pacing up and down, and finally, almost defiantly, he made up his mind to open the cupboard. He had already washed the glass in the enamel drinking fountain. Now he rinsed it again and poured a tot of brandy into it.

"Would you care for a drop of this?"

"No thanks."

Albert Jorisse was finding it hard to keep awake. His cheeks were flushed, and Maigret was sure his eyes were smarting. From time to time he swayed in his chair.

"Eventually, I daresay, you'll prove yourself to be a man."

He could hear footsteps in the corridor, those of a man and a woman, and he knew that it was Monique accompanied by Lucas. He had a decision to make. That was what he had been brooding over for the last quarter of an hour. Should he have the girl brought into his office, or should he interview her next door?

With a little shrug, he went across and opened the door. Both of them had drops of rain glistening on their shoulders. Monique was no longer her old confident self, and when she caught sight of Albert she stopped dead in her tracks, clutched her bag more tightly, and glared furiously at the Chief Superintendent.

"Did you take her to see a doctor?"

"At first she flatly refused to go. I . . ."

"What did he find?"

Jorisse stood up and seemed on the point of groveling at her feet to beg her forgiveness.

"Nothing."

"You mean she's not pregnant?"

"She never has been."

Jorisse, hardly able to believe his ears, didn't know which way to turn. He made a sudden move as if to spring at Maigret, whom he seemed to regard as the cruelest man on earth.

Maigret, after shutting the door, indicated a chair to the young woman.

"Have you anything to say?"

"I did believe . . ."

"No."

"What do you know about it? You're not a woman."

Then, turning to the young man:

"I swear to you, Albert, that I truly believed I was going to have a child."

Maigret, unmoved but not wishing to be unfair, said:

"For how long?"

"For several days."

"And then?"

"When I discovered it was a false alarm, I didn't want him to be disappointed."

"Disappointed?"

Maigret exchanged glances with Lucas. The two of them went out together into the adjoining office. They shut the door, leaving the young lovers to themselves.

"As soon as I spoke about taking her to a doctor I could see that there was something amiss. She protested violently. It wasn't until I threatened to arrest her and Albert . . ."

Maigret was not listening. Lucas was not telling him anything he didn't already know. Torrence was back at his desk.

"Did you do what I asked?"

"They're working on the list. It's going to be a long one. For the last two years or more, Chief Superintendent Antoine and his squad have been plugging away at the cases. Apparently . . ."

Maigret went over to the connecting door and put his ear to it.

"What are they up to?" asked Lucas.

"Nothing."

"Are they talking?"

"They're not saying a word."

He decided to look in on the Chief Commissioner and bring him up to date. They talked for a while about this and that. Maigret spent the next hour or so dropping in on various colleagues for a chat.

When he returned to his office, Albert and Monique looked as if they had not stirred during his absence. They were still sitting upright on their chairs, ten feet or so apart. The girl's face was unrevealing, her jaw, which was so like her mother's and aunts', resolutely set.

Whenever her eyes chanced to meet the young man's, it was hard to tell whether there was more contempt or loathing in her glance.

As for Jorisse, he was utterly crushed. His eyes were red, either with exhaustion or with weeping.

"You are both free to go," Maigret said, without preamble, as he went toward his chair.

It was Monique who asked:

"Will there be anything in the papers?"

"There's no reason why there should be."

"Will my mother have to be told?"

"I don't think that will be necessary."

"And my employers?"

He shook his head, and she got swiftly to her feet and made for the door, without sparing so much as a glance for Jorisse. With her hand on the doorknob, she turned to the Chief Superintendent and said:

"You knew all along, didn't you?"

"Yes," he replied. Then, with a sigh, he said to Albert:

"You're free to go, as well."

And, seeing that the youngster did not stir:

"You'd better hurry, if you want to catch up with her . . ."

She was already on the stairs.

"Should I, do you think?"

"What did she say to you?"

"She called me an idiot."

"Is that all?"

"She added that on no account would she ever let me speak to her again."

"And then?"

"Nothing. I don't know."

"As I've already said, you're free to go."

"What shall I say to my parents?"

"Whatever you like. They'll be only too delighted to have you back."

"Do you really think so?"

In the end, Maigret almost had to push him out. He still seemed to have something on his mind.

"Off you go, you young idiot!"

"I'm not a ruffian, then?"

"No, only an idiot! She was quite right."

He turned his head away, sniffed, and murmured:

"Thanks."

Presently, alone in his office at last, Maigret was able to pour himself another drop of brandy.

CHAPTER NINE

JUDGE COMÉLIAU GROWS RESTIVE

☐ "Is that you, Maigret?"

"Yes, Judge."

He telephoned every day, and if one of Maigret's colleagues happened to be in the room at the time Maigret would give him a wink. His voice sounded unusually bland when he talked to the Examining Magistrate.

"How are things on the Thouret front?"

"Progressing! Progressing!"

"Don't you think it's been dragging on a bit too long?"

"You know how it is with a crime of this sort. It takes time to clear things up."

"Are you sure it's a case of thieves falling out?"

"You've said so yourself, right from the start. Your words were:

" 'It's as plain as a pikestaff.' "

"Do you believe this Schrameck fellow's story?"

"I'm convinced he was telling the truth."

"In that case, who did kill Louis Thouret?"

"Someone who wanted his money."

"At any rate, do the best you can to speed things up."

"You have my word on that, Judge."

He did nothing about it, however, but, instead, turned his attention to two other cases, which kept him busy for most of the day. Three men, Janvier and young Lapointe among them, were taking turns keeping an eye on the house in Rue d'Angoulême twenty-four hours a day. The telephone was still being tapped.

He was no longer interested either in Madame Thouret or in her daughter. Jorisse, too, who was once more working full time at the bookshop on Boulevard Saint-Michel, had been eliminated from the case. It was as if he had never known them.

As for the theft, he had turned the file over to his colleague Antoine, who was having Jef the Clown, alias the Acrobat, brought up for questioning nearly every day. Maigret occasionally ran into Jef in the corridor.

"Everything okay?"

"Everything's fine, Chief Superintendent."

The weather was cold but dry. The proprietress of the house in Rue d'Angoulême had not been able to find any other tenants, so two of her rooms were still vacant. As for the three girls who were still living there, they knew that the house was being watched and no longer dared ply their usual trade. They hardly ever went out, except to have a meal in a nearby restaurant or to buy something at the delicatessen, or when one of them went to a movie.

"What do they do with themselves all day?" Maigret asked Janvier, when things had been going on like this for several days.

"They sleep, or play cards or patience. One of them, the one they call Arlette, sticks her tongue out at me every time she sees me from the window. Yesterday she tried something different. She hitched up her dressing gown and showed me her behind."

The mobile squad in Marseilles had taken over the inquiries concerning the knife. They were searching not only in the town itself, but in the surrounding villages as well. They were also taking an interest in any shady local character who had recently moved to Paris.

All these routine inquiries were being conducted unhurriedly and without fuss. And yet Maigret had not forgotten Monsieur Louis. Once, when he had to go to Rue de Clignancourt on other business, he even went so far as to look in on Mademoiselle Léone, not forgetting to buy a cream cake for the old lady on his way.

"Have you still not solved the mystery?"

"Sooner or later the truth will come to light."

He said nothing to the former secretary about Monsieur Louis's activities.

"Do you know why he was killed?"

"For his money."

"Surely he can't have had that much!"

"He had a very large income."

"Poor man! What a shame to have to die just when all his troubles were over."

He did not venture the long climb up to Monsieur Saimbron's apartment, but ran across him by chance one day in the Flower Market. They exchanged greetings.

Then one morning, at long last, he received a telephone call from Marseilles. It lasted a long time. Afterward, he went up to the Registry and was there for nearly an hour, looking through hundreds of registration forms. Then he went downstairs to Records, where he spent nearly as long again.

It was around eleven when he went out into the courtyard and got into one of the little Headquarters cars.

"Rue d'Angoulême."

It was young Lapointe who was on guard outside the house.

"Everyone at home?"

"Only one of them is out. She's doing her shopping around the neighborhood."

"Which one?"

"Olga. She's the dark one."

He rang the bell. The curtains twitched. Mariette Gibon, the landlady, flip-flapped to the door in her bedroom slippers.

"Well, well! If it isn't the Big White Chief himself! Your men must be getting fed up with wearing down the pavement outside my door."

"Is Arlette at home?"

"Shall I call her down?"

"No, thanks. I'd rather go up to her room."

She stayed out in the entrance lobby, looking uneasy, and he went upstairs and knocked at the door on the second floor.

"Come in."

As usual, she was in her dressing gown, lying on the unmade bed reading a romantic novel.

"Oh! So it's you."

"In person," he said, putting his hat on the chest of drawers and sitting down on a chair by the bed.

She seemed both surprised and amused.

"Don't tell me you're still going on about that same old business?"

"The case will not be closed until the murderer is found."

"You don't mean you still haven't found him? I thought you were such a cunning old fox. I hope it doesn't embarrass you, me being in my dressing gown like this."

"Not in the least."

"I daresay you must be used to it by now."

Without stirring from the bed, she moved so that her dressing gown fell open. When Maigret seemed not to notice, she said provocatively:

"What do you say to this?"

"What?"

"Seeing all this."

When he still remained impassive, she made a vulgar gesture and said impatiently:

"How about it?"

"Thanks."

"Yes thanks, do you mean?"

"No thanks."

"Well, really, old man . . . You are the . . ."

"Do you get a kick out of being coarse?"

"You're surely not going to lecture me, on top of everything else?"

All the same, she wrapped the dressing gown around herself again and sat up on the edge of the bed.

"What exactly is it you want with me?"

"Do your parents know that you are no longer working in Avenue Matignon?"

"What are you getting at now?"

"You worked for a year at Chez Hélène et Hélène in Avenue Matignon."

"What of it?"

"I was just wondering if your father knew you'd changed your occupation."

"What business is it of yours?"

"Your father is a good man."

"He's an old fool, and that's a fact."

"If he should ever find out what you've been up to . . ."

"Are you thinking of telling him?"

"I might."

This time, she was unable to conceal her agitation.

"You haven't been to Clermont-Ferrand to see my parents?"

"Not yet . . ."

She got up, made a dash for the door, and flung it open, to reveal Mariette Gibon, who had obviously been standing there for some time with her ear glued to the door panel.

"My God! You've got a nerve!"

"May I come in?"

"No. Shove off. And if I ever catch you spying again . . ."

Maigret had not moved from his chair.

"Well?" he said.

"Well, what? I can't think what you want from me."

"You know perfectly well."

"No, I don't. You'll have to spell it out."

"You've been living in this house for the past six months."

"So what?"

"You hardly ever go out in the daytime, so you must know most of what goes on here."

"Well?"

"There's one person who used to be a regular visitor, but who hasn't set foot in the house since Monsieur Louis's death."

Her pupils seemed to contract.

Once again she went to the door, but there was no one behind it.

"Well, anyway, he didn't come here to see me."

"Who, then?"

"You must know the answer to that. I think I'd better get dressed."

"Why?"

"Because after this little talk of ours I'll be safer out of this house."

She let her dressing gown slip to the floor, but this time with no thought of being provocative. Then she snatched up a bra and a pair of panties, and opened the wardrobe.

"I might have known that this was how it would end."

She was talking to herself.

"You're a clever bastard, I'll say that for you."

"Arresting criminals is my job."

"Have you arrested him?"

She had taken a black dress from the wardrobe and now had it on. She proceeded to daub her mouth with lipstick.

"Not yet."

"But you do know who he is?"

"You are going to tell me."

"You seem very sure of yourself."

He took his wallet out of his pocket and extracted a photograph of a man. He was about thirty, and there was a scar on his left temple. She glanced at the photograph, but said nothing.

"Is that him?"

"You seem to think so."

"Am I wrong?"

"Where can I go to be safe while he's still on the loose?"

"I'll arrange for one of my inspectors to look after you."

"Which one?"

"Which would you prefer?"

"The dark one with lots of hair."

"That's Inspector Lapointe."

Returning to the subject of the photograph, Maigret asked:

"What do you know about Marco?"

"That he was the landlady's lover. Do we have to talk here?"

"Where is he now?"

Without replying, she began stuffing all her clothes and personal possessions into a large suitcase. She couldn't wait to get out of the house, it seemed.

"We can finish this conversation somewhere else."

And, as he bent down to pick up her suitcase, she added:

"Well, well! So you can be chivalrous when you want to!"

The door of the downstairs sitting room was open. Mariette Gibon was standing in the doorway, looking drawn and anxious.

"Where are you going?"

"Wherever the Chief Superintendent is taking me."

"Is she under arrest?"

She didn't dare question them further. She watched them go out, and then she went to the window and raised the curtain a little. Maigret pushed the suitcase into the back of the car and said to Lapointe:

"I'll send someone along to relieve you. As soon as he arrives, come and join us at the Brasserie de la République."

"Right you are, Chief."

He gave instructions to the driver, but did not get in the car.

"Let's go."

"To the Brasserie de la République?"

"For the time being, yes."

It was only a few hundred yards away. They sat down at a table at the back of the room.

"I have to make a phone call. Take my word for it, it will be better for you if you don't try to give me the slip."

"I understand."

He telephoned the Quai, to give instructions to Torrence. When he got back to the table, he ordered two apéritifs.

"Where is Marco?"

"I don't know. After you came to the house that first time, the landlady told me to phone him and tell him not to try to get in touch with her until he heard from her again."

"When did you give him that message?"

"Half an hour after you left. I called from a restaurant on Boulevard Voltaire."

"Did you actually speak to him?"

"No. I left a message with one of the waiters in a bar in Rue de Douai."

"Do you know his name?"

"Félix."

"And the name of the bar?"

"Le Poker d'As."

"Hasn't she heard anything from him since?"

"No. She's going through hell. She's not blind to the fact that she's twenty years older than he is, and she's forever imagining him chasing girls."

"Is he the one who's got the money?"

"I don't know. But he was in the house that day."

"What day?"

"The Monday that Monsieur Louis was murdered."

"What time did he get to Rue d'Angoulême?"

"About five. He and the landlady went and shut themselves up in her room."

"Did she at any time go into Monsieur Louis's room?"

"She may have. I didn't notice. He left after about an hour. I heard the door slam behind him."

"Didn't she attempt to get in touch with him again through one of you girls?"

"She was afraid we might be followed."

"Did she know that the telephone was being tapped?"

"She wasn't fooled by that business of your pipe. She's

quick on the uptake. I don't like her much, but she's really rather pathetic. She's absolutely crazy about him. It's making her ill."

Young Lapointe found them sitting contentedly over their drinks.

"What will you have?"

The girl was looking Lapointe over from head to foot and smiling. Lapointe was studiously avoiding her eyes.

"The same as you."

"I want you to take her to some quiet little hotel and book a couple of adjoining rooms with a door between them. You're not to let her out of your sight until I give you the word. As soon as you're settled in, call and let me know where you are. You shouldn't have to go very far. They might have rooms at the Hôtel Moderne just across from here. I'd rather she didn't talk to anyone. You'd better arrange to have her meals sent up to her room."

When she and Lapointe went off together, it looked to Maigret as if she were taking him into custody, rather than the other way around.

The search continued for another two days. Someone— no one ever found out who—must have tipped off Félix, the barman in Rue de Douai. At any rate, he had gone into hiding with a friend and was not traced until the following night.

It took the greater part of the night to get him to admit that he knew Marco and to persuade him to reveal his whereabouts.

Marco had left Paris and taken a room in a country inn on the banks of the Seine mainly patronized by anglers. At this time of year he had the place all to himself.

Before the police could disarm him, he fired two shots. Mercifully, no one was hurt. He had the money stolen from

Monsieur Louis in a money belt that had probably been made for him by Mariette Gibon.

"Is that you, Maigret?"

"Yes, Judge."

"How are things progressing in the Thouret case?"

"It's all over. I'll be handing the murderer and his accomplice over to you very shortly."

"Who are they? Shady characters, as we thought?"

"They couldn't be shadier. The woman runs a bawdy house, and the man is a thug from Marseilles. Monsieur Louis was fool enough to hide the money on top of the wardrobe and . . ."

"What's that you said . . . ?"

"He couldn't possibly be allowed to find out that the money was gone. Marco saw to that. We've found the shop where he bought the knife. My report will be on your desk by tonight . . ."

This was always the most boring part. Maigret spent all afternoon writing, the tip of his tongue sticking out like a schoolboy's.

It wasn't until after dinner that night that he suddenly remembered Arlette and young Lapointe.

"Damn! There's something I forgot to do," he exclaimed.

"Is it important?" asked Madame Maigret.

"Not that important, come to think of it. It's so late. I might as well leave it till morning. Let's go to bed."

September 19, 1952